WORSHIP ME

MEN OF INKED BOOK SEVEN

www.chellebliss.com

CHELLE BLISS

USA TODAY BESTSELLING AUTHOR

Proofread by Fiona Wilson of Fiona's Dreaming
Cover Design © Chelle Bliss
Formatted by Chelle Bliss
Cover Models Alfie Gordillo & Colleen McMahon
Cover Photo © Eric Battershell Photography

IZZY

"Izzy, please. Be reasonable."

I loved when James begged. "Say it again," I taunted him.

What the fuck with the be reasonable comment? I'm always reasonable. Okay, maybe that isn't entirely true. I usually shoot from the hip and save the apologies for later. My big mouth has gotten me into more trouble over the years, and much of it I try to forget, especially when it comes to James.

He arched an eyebrow, and the same

shitty smirk I'd grown accustomed to flashed across his lips. "I could make you say yes."

"Doubtful." I glared at him, feeling supercocky even though I was in no position to be.

James, my loving husband of over ten years, decided that tonight was a good time to tie me to the bed. I should've known he was up to no good because it'd been more than a little bit since he'd used restraints during sex. I figured we were just getting our kink on and that he wanted to try something new, but nope, the bastard knew I wouldn't like what he was asking and made sure I didn't have an out.

"Baby," he whispered, running his thumbs across my bottom lip and trying to seduce me. "You know you can't say no to me. Never have and never will."

There were very few people in this world that could make me do anything, but James had a power over me since the first night I met him. Saying no to him had always been damn near impossible, and I almost hated myself because of it.

I never wanted to be that girl—the one who caved to anything her husband asked. Never in my life had I wanted to be her, an easy mark and a carpet for her husband to walk all over, but things don't always turn out the way we plan. I learned that the hard way.

James wasn't even on my radar until the night of Joe and Suzy's wedding when he sauntered in with his good looks and charm. The arrogant bastard seemed to work me like he'd known me my entire life, and I fell for it.

I thought I'd won when I snuck out. I figured I'd never see him again, so what did it matter. Boy, was I wrong.

"I've said no to you plenty of times." I refused to let him use his sexual prowess, which I'd done in the past, but sometimes I had to dig my heels in and find my inner bitch.

I pulled at the restraints and tried to break free, but it was useless. The man could tie the most wicked knots, and it had been years since I'd been able to wiggle out of them. Every time I escaped, he'd learn a new technique until he found just the right one to render me helpless.

His lips scorched a path down my neck, and my back arched as if begging for his touch. "Say yes, Izzy."

I stifled the moan that formed low in my throat, but I squeaked instead when he sucked my nipple into his mouth. My body rocked on its own, moving toward him instinctively, wanting the bite of his teeth. His hand slid down my front, cupping my pussy, not hard enough to give me pleasure, only the sweet torment that he reveled in.

"Say yes, and I'll give you what you want."

He was playing with me. James was a master manipulator. I didn't know if it was his background with the DEA or just something he was born with, but he used it perfectly when it suited his purpose.

I clenched my jaw, grinding my teeth together. "No."

He wanted me to go to Miami to help gather information on a case and spend a few days with his parents. I loved them. I had every intention of saying yes, but saying no made everything more interesting.

He pulled my panties to the side before dipping two fingers inside me with the most sinful smile. "Last chance, baby," he warned.

What was he going to do to me if I didn't give in? The thought passed through my mind, but I pushed it away. I was lost in the feel of his hands on my skin and the ache between my legs, but my resistance held. "No," I bit out.

He peered up, my nipple still in his mouth, smiling around the tip. The goddamn smile. I knew it so well, and we'd been together so long, I knew I was in for something I wasn't going to like.

He thrust his fingers through my wetness and curled them, pressing against my G-spot.

The sensation made me almost breathless and made me want to say yes to him without a second thought, but then he bit down on my nipple, and I was shocked back to reality and the knowledge that this was just a game to him.

Involuntarily, my back arched off the bed, offering my breast to him. My body had always betrayed me when it came to him. It was like he had the power to short-circuit my wiring and reprogram me, and there wasn't a damn thing I could do to change it.

He added a third finger, filling me so completely that I moaned my pleasure and cried out his name. As if he'd achieved his goal, he pulled his fingers out and rubbed the wetness over my clit, taunting me. Slowly, his fingertips circled my supersensitive bud, driving me closer to the edge. It hit me. The bastard was going to torture me, denying me the orgasm I so badly wanted and now needed until I said yes and gave him what he wanted. This wasn't about sex or connection. It was about getting what James wanted, and this was the only way he knew how.

I wiggled my bottom, trying to stop him before it was too late… But I'd already passed the point of no return, and he damn well knew it. His fingers were skilled, his mind sharp and cunning, and he was the master of my body.

My toes curled, the orgasm just within reach as his teeth clamped down harder against my nipple, pushing me closer to the edge. Just as my body tensed, losing myself in oblivion, James's touch vanished.

"Fucking asshole," I hissed and glared down my body at my sadistic husband.

He smiled, licking my wetness from his fingers with the deepest, sexiest moan I'd ever heard. I yanked at the restraints, again trying to break free because I wanted to launch myself across the bed and wrap my hands around his neck. Who the hell was I kidding? I'd rather knock his ass down and sit on his face, letting him slowly suffocate while getting the orgasm he was so intent on denying me.

"I'm going to let you think about your answer." His tongue swept across his beautiful full lips, making sure he'd captured every drop of me.

He was completely naked, every muscle on his perfectly chiseled body glistening in the candlelight I'd spent a half hour lighting before he got home from work. My parents had the boys for the weekend and I didn't want to waste a moment of our alone time, but in no way had I ever thought this was how our night would turn out.

"You can't leave me like this," I pleaded, but I knew the man was just as stubborn as I was, so I was basically screwed. "Come on. We're alone for the first time in months, and you're going to just walk out?"

James let out a vicious laugh. "You want this, baby?" He wrapped his hand around his cock, pumping it roughly.

I inhaled and closed my eyes, choking

down the scream that so badly wanted to break loose along with a million ways to tell him to go fuck himself. "I want to come, sweetie." My voice was anything but sweet as I said the words.

He gripped his cock harder, moaning and putting on a show for me.

My gaze dipped to his cock. "You wouldn't dare."

He arched an eyebrow and accepted my challenge, pumping so fast that I could almost feel him thrusting into me. He placed his feet shoulder-width apart and tipped his head back, giving me an unobstructed view as he jacked himself off.

My pussy throbbed with each thrust, and I silently cursed him for making me watch. I couldn't help but feel the wetness between my legs start to run down my ass crack. I squeezed my thighs together, trying to quell the ache, but it was futile. What I needed wouldn't be fixed without his touch.

James stepped closer, and I licked my lips. "You want this cock?"

I didn't dare speak. I couldn't. The only thing I wanted to say was yes and then beg him to fuck me, to finish me off and give me the relief I so badly needed. I wouldn't give him the satisfaction of letting him know how desperately I wanted to get off. He knew, though. The bastard always did. But I wasn't going to say the words.

I didn't beg.

It wasn't in my nature, even when it came to my husband.

"It's so hard, Izzy."

Man, he was pulling out the asshole card…big-time.

He smirked and moved closer, almost within kicking range. "You want me to fuck that beautiful cunt of yours?"

His hand stroked faster as I lay there help-less and panting. I shook my head and bit down on my lip to keep myself quiet. The dull ache between my legs turned almost painful, and I was unable to escape.

All day I'd worked myself up, planning for a night of crazy sex with him, like we used to have before the kids started growing up and work took over our lives.

Private nights alone didn't happen often enough anymore, and now he was going to waste it taunting me until I gave in to him.

The bed dipped, and I thought I had been victorious as he climbed between my legs. In my mind, I was already doing the victory lap and waving the checkered flag, but my celebration didn't last long.

"You know I don't need pretty things like this." He kneeled before me, pumping his cock with one hand, and tangled his fingers in the waistband of my panties. I'd bought them special for tonight, thinking I needed to spice up our sex life, even though James preferred me naked. "I want what's underneath." Before I could protest, he ripped the material from my body and tossed the shards to the floor.

"Take it," I said. My voice was laced with so much need and want that I sounded pathetic even to myself. No one, and I mean no one, got to me like he did. Maybe that's why I married him. God knew, it wasn't because of his manners. The man was a beast in the sack and the best verbal sparring partner I'd ever had.

He leaned forward, placing his mouth over my clit. *Sweet Jesus.* Right there. It was like the clouds had parted on a rainy day and the sun shone down, bathing me in warmth. I pushed the back of my head into the pillow, closing my eyes and thrusting my cunt into his face. Just a little more. I needed more of him. A flick of the tongue. The tease of his teeth. Something to push me over the edge and to ignite the slow burn that was overtaking my ability to think or speak.

My entire body was on fire, needing the release so badly that he'd denied me minutes earlier. His tongue swiped against my clit, and my entire body quaked with pleasure. *Right there. Oh God. Right there.* I moaned, unable to hold it in, thankful for the brilliant moves his tongue made against my pussy.

I'm so close…fuck. So close. My muscles were strained and my breathing was erratic and I started to sweat. My toes curled, the sign that it was about to happen—that I was about to have an orgasm that would tear me apart and send me into the best post-sex blackout of my life.

"Yes!" I chanted. "Yes."

Then nothing.

My eyes flew open just as he leaped off the bed in one quick move, like an Olympic gymnast going for the gold in the bullshit pommel horse event.

"James." He was lucky I was tied up because I would've ripped his cock right off out of anger and frustration and let him watch me fuck myself with it.

He licked his lips, wiping them clean of

my wetness again. "I'm going to go get something to drink. I'm feeling parched." He gave me a mischievous smile. "You relax for a little bit."

Parched? He didn't know parched, but he would. The man was about to have a dry spell that would make the Mojave Desert look like the wettest place on earth. I wouldn't forget this night anytime soon, and I'd make sure he didn't either.

"James," I yelled, pulling at the restraints and twisting in the bed as he started to walk to the doorway. "You can*not* leave me like *this*."

He stared at me for a minute, watching me as I tried to break free…still with that cocky grin. He glanced down, catching sight of the leftover black rope he'd tossed aside earlier. "You're right." He stalked toward me after grabbing the rope off the floor and cinching it.

Fuck. Me and my big mouth. Why did I always do this shit to myself? I couldn't have just let him walk out the door and figured something out myself, not now. He was about to spread me out, making sure I wouldn't be able to squeeze my legs together enough times to get myself off without him.

I started to kick my feet as he moved closer, flailing on the bed because I knew what he was going to do. "Please don't."

But James was stronger, and no matter how hard I kicked, I wasn't going to win. He snatched my foot in midair, slipping the rope around my ankle, and secured it to the bedpost without missing a beat. "This is for your own good," he said. "I don't want you to hurt yourself trying to break free."

What a crock of shit. My glare turned into something deeper and angrier. "I'm going to make you pay for this."

He tipped his head back and laughed before he grabbed my only free foot easily, which was moving around in wild, uneven circles. "I look forward to the payback, love. You can end this, you know," he said, standing at my side, and stared down at me with the biggest hard-on.

I closed my eyes. I needed to avoid his penetrating stare and the rock-hard, velvety smooth dick that was only inches from me. "Fuck you, Jimmy."

I could do this. I could outlast him. I mean, we always played rough, and orgasm deprivation had been our thing for a while. But that was back in the day when we were banging like we were the last two humans on earth trying to repopulate the world. Think of something other than sex. I needed to focus on something besides the ache between my legs and the wetness running over my asshole, but it was like trying to ignore the single drip of water outside my bedroom window after a rainstorm.

"You always have to be a hardhead." His hot breath skidded across my face as he leaned over, and his cock pressed against my arm. "Just remember, this is your choice, not mine." His hand slid down my front, cupping my mound.

The tips of his fingers penetrated my pussy and made my need so much worse. I wanted to cry out, beg for him to give me the orgasm he'd denied me twice. I thought he'd change his mind and that maybe he'd give me what I wanted, but just as that delusion went through my mind, he pulled his hand away.

Thwack! I jolted off the mattress, the throb growing more intense at the pain and pleasure mix of his swat.

A lesser woman would cave, begging to come and giving her husband whatever he wanted. But that wouldn't be me. It wasn't my way. I'd always take the hardest, most fucked-up path, and James knew it. The bastard always used my personality against me.

But I'd be lying if I said I hated him. I'd never loved another man the way I completely and utterly loved my husband. A lesser, weaker man wouldn't have been able to deal with my bullshit and attitude. That's why we worked. Not because he handled me, but because we brought out the best in each other.

Maybe not in that moment as I was tied to the bed, splayed open while he worked me up to the point that I was ready to break.

I opened my mouth to speak, to scream, to beg, but his footsteps had grown quiet and farther away. I sucked in a breath and tried to steady my breathing. He was fucking leaving me here, tied down, alone and aching for an orgasm. He didn't like to lose as much as I didn't like to give in. I had a hard decision to make—cave in and finally say yes, or most likely lie here all night without the ability to move.

He was a fucker sometimes, but he was my fucker. Once I heard the familiar creak of the last step on the stairway, I opened my eyes and stared at the ceiling, trying to think of anything except the throbbing need I had between my legs.

Nothing worked.

No matter what I tried to think about, it

did nothing to lessen the want. The sting from his palm stayed for far too long, almost making me mindless and wanton.

I don't know how long I lay there with no clock in the room, staring at the ceiling and going through the motions of Lamaze because it helped during childbirth and maybe it could work wonders in this situation.

An eternity passed before he came back, still naked and devastatingly handsome. "Ready?" he asked from the foot of the bed, cock still hard and taunting me as it moved.

"No." I stared at the ceiling, keeping my eyes off his cock and his face.

It didn't bother me in the slightest that I was spread wide, laid out before him like a toy he could fuck with all night. James had seen and explored every inch of my body, and there was nothing to be shy or bashful about. I, in turn, had done the same to him.

I knew every crevice, every birthmark, and dip to his muscles. We were one in that. We were the yin to the other's yang and completed each other so freakishly well that if I weren't in our relationship, I'd make myself sick from the perfectness.

"You're being ridiculous."

Did he really just say that to me?

Those were fighting words. The man knew better than to mutter that sentence to me. But he went there anyway. What started out as a game, because I liked to play hard to get, was turning into something wickeder.

I had two options—let it go and say yes to his simple request, or dig my heels in and not get off tonight and possibly tomorrow.

My mind was telling me to be an asshole and not give in, but my pussy was screaming for me to just say yes and end the misery.

I let my gaze wander up his body, taking all of him in, and in a moment of weakness, I let my cunt answer for me. "I'll go to Miami to see your parents with you," I said, almost choking on the words because I couldn't believe I'd actually given in. The words were foreign on my tongue and tasted salty.

James looked so satisfied as he smiled down at me. "Thank you."

"Don't speak." Normally, I'd be angry with myself, but I was so damned turned on that I didn't even care anymore. I just wanted his cock, his hands, his mouth, and all of him on and in me. "Just fuck me before I change my mind."

Thankfully, he listened. James climbed onto the bed, nestling between my legs before thrusting into me. I cried out as he pummeled me, slamming his body against mine. When the orgasm crashed over me, it didn't feel like defeat—because it was the best damn orgasm of my life.

2

IZZY

"Mommy. Mommy," Trace yelled, running through my parents' house to leap into my arms.

I hugged him tightly as he wrapped his legs around my body and locked his arms around my neck, almost putting me in a choke hold. The little man had no idea how strong he was, just like his daddy. "I missed you too, baby. Did you have fun?"

He brought his mouth close to my ear and whispered, "Nonna took us for ice cream."

"Butter pecan?"

He looked me square in the face with his eyebrows turned inward and grimaced. "Mint chocolate chip. Pecan is gross, Ma."

"Right." I laughed. "Where are your brothers?"

"Outside playing with Gigi and Lily." He untangled his body from mine and shimmied down to the ground. "I gotta go watch the Cubs with Grandpa."

James walked in after finishing a phone call just as Trace ran back into the living room. "Where did he run off to?"

"Cubs are on."

"Enough said," James replied, kicking off his boots before we walked into the kitchen to greet my mother.

"Ah," Ma said, holding out her arms to us like she hadn't just seen us two days ago. "You two look well-rested."

"I kept her in bed most of the weekend," James said, moving in front of me to embrace her as she laughed. "Thank you for taking the kids off our hands for a few nights."

She probably had no idea that he meant he'd kept me tied to the bed and not served breakfast in bed like a queen. But then again, knowing my mom, she probably suspected. "They were lovely. Soon they'll be too old to hang out with Grandma."

"They'll always love you," I reminded her. I remembered spending time with my grandparents, but as soon as I became a teenager, my weekends were spent with friends instead of them. I looked back on it now and regretted all the moments I missed.

Suzy strolled in from the living room and leaned against the counter next to me. "What can I help with? I can't sit and watch baseball for another minute."

"Are they losing?" I asked her.

"No, but bases are loaded, and the guys are stressing me out."

James hugged me from behind and kissed my neck. "I'm going to go sit with the guys and bullshit."

I patted his hand and leaned into his lips. "Have fun."

As soon as he walked out of the room, Max, Angel, and Mia walked in, and we all started to get to work, but this week would be easier. Ma had already prepped the breaded chicken, and the pasta was lasagna. There would be no slaving over a hot stove this weekend.

"How about after dinner us girls go shopping?" Ma asked as she closed the oven door for the chicken and lasagna to cook.

"I could use some retail therapy," Aunt Fran said, wandering into the kitchen as soon as Ma said the word shopping.

"Sounds like the best idea ever," I said, and Max, Mia, Angel and Suzy agreed.

"Let's get the table set, and we'll leave the guys to clean up." Ma laughed and held her belly. "I'm sure they can do it once."

I loved each of them, but when it came to doing the Sunday dishes, they somehow became allergic to water. The only day they got off their asses was Mother's Day.

"They should be doing it every week," Max said, thinking the same thing we all did.

"You're cute, Max," Mia said sarcastically and motioned toward Ma with her head. "She ruined 'em."

"I did no such thing. They were my babies, and now they're your men. If they're ruined, you only have one person to blame."

Joe strolled in, sliding his arms around Suzy's waist. "Need any help?"

All eyes in the room turned to Suzy. "We have this, baby, but do you think you guys can clean up for us? We have something we need to do."

He kissed her neck. "We'll get it. You ladies work too much and deserve a weekend off."

Everyone stood there in shock and completely silent. That was classic Joe. He was the least lazy one of the bunch. He had the asshole gene too, but not when it came to the women in his life. For us, he'd do anything. But if you were a prick and hassled one of us or anyone in the family, Joe would make you wish you had never been born.

"Well, I…" Max stammered as Joe walked out of the room just as quietly and quickly as he entered. "God, sometimes I hate you, Suzy. You're a lucky little whore."

Suzy shrugged with a small laugh. "What can I say? I hit the jackpot."

Max let out a tiny growl. "You and your good girl 'I can't cook worth shit' act really paid off."

"Oh, shush it," I told Max, hitting her with my hip as I walked by. "Let's get the food on the table so we can go spend some cash."

FOUR HOURS LATER, WE WALKED BACK INTO my parents' with so many bags it looked like we'd cleared out the entire mall.

"Jesus." Anthony met us in the foyer with

his mouth hanging open. "What the hell did you get?"

"They were having a sale," Max barked as she set her bags down on the floor. "Problem?" She quirked an eyebrow, and with the look on her face, not even I would fuck with her.

"None. But there better be something sexy in there." Anthony smiled and started rummaging through the bags.

She swatted his hands. "Get your paws off. You can't see until we get home."

"I like the sound of that." Anthony smirked.

"Out of the way. Coming through," Ma said, heading straight up the staircase with her bags. She stopped at the landing and looked down at us. "I'll be right back, and we'll have dessert."

"I'm exhausted after that," Suzy said, pulling her hair back into a tight ponytail before wiping her forehead with the back of her hand. "You ladies shop like it's a race."

"We're back," I yelled toward the living room, but the guys were too busy watching sports to even care.

They were probably exhausted from cleaning up the dinner after we ditched them as soon as our plates were in the sink. James was like Joe and didn't make a peep when we told them we were heading to the mall. It didn't matter if he grumbled, I was still going anyway.

"Get anything new for our trip?" James asked as I stored the bags in the first-floor office that was now more a kids' playroom.

"I got a few sexy things." I held out the bags to him, excited about the few items I could find. "Wanna look?"

"Why don't you put on a fashion show for me later after the boys go to sleep?" He grabbed my ass and pulled me against him. "I didn't get enough of you last night. I need more."

"You never have enough," I reminded

him, reaching down and grabbing him by the balls. "It's why I own you."

He ground his cock against me, inching his knee between my legs. "Baby," he said, rubbing his thigh against my clit. "We own each other."

3

JAMES

I SCRUBBED MY HANDS DOWN MY FACE AND glanced at the clock for at least the fifth time in the last hour. The day seemed to be dragging, and I hadn't even made it to the afternoon yet. Mondays always sucked. After two blissful days at home, which wasn't usually the case on a weekend, the last place I wanted to be was at work.

After a weekend filled with more sex than I'd had in years, every muscle in my body ached. It was worth every ounce of pain to fuck my wife like we did before we had the kids, the complete cockblockers that they usually were. I loved my children, don't get me wrong. They were the light of my life and all that shit that Hallmark puts on the greeting cards. But damn it if they didn't ruin more orgasms than I have fingers. I swear the little bastards—I use that term in the nicest way—came programmed with a "my parents are fucking, so I need to go interrupt" gene. Someday, they'd realize the agony they put me through when they had their own wives—and children cockblocking them.

Thomas made a grand appearance, showing up at the office two hours late and looking just as shitty as I felt. "We didn't get to talk about it yesterday, but how did the talk with Izzy go?"

I couldn't be completely honest with him. I wasn't stupid. Being married to his sister did complicate things at times. The man would probably have my balls in a vise if he knew half the shit I pulled with her.

He knew about our kink because he knew that side of my life before I ever claimed his sister as my own, but it wasn't something we freely discussed—and I wasn't about to start doing it now. There were certain topics that were off-limits, and that was certainly one.

"It went really well." I couldn't look him in the eye as I lied through my teeth. "She's on board."

The ending went great, and the middle was amazing, but the start of the weekend didn't go exactly as I'd planned. I thought Izzy would say yes to my simple request and that we'd have a kick-ass fuckfest all weekend, but she had to draw it out and dig her goddamn heels in, making it a little more difficult. Not that I minded. Sexually tormenting my wife was almost like a sport to me, and I loved every minute of it. Just thinking about the way she wiggled and pulled against the restraints while completely naked and open made me hard.

"Izzy said yes?"

I kept typing, pretending to be too en-grossed in the message on my screen to look up. "Yep."

"That's great, man. When do you guys leave?"

When he moved on to something other than my weekend activities, I leaned back in my chair and finally looked him in the eyes. "In a few days. As soon as I can get her out the door. But you know how that goes."

That was easier said than done. Izzy could easily be mistaken for a Kardashian with the amount of luggage she brought even for a weekend getaway. The woman was ready for everything. Heels, dresses, shorts, boots…you name it, it was in her suitcase. It was more like a minimum of three suitcases that were bursting at the seams with so much shit that she couldn't possibly wear it all in a month even if she tried. And trust me, she has tried just to prove her point, but she's failed.

"It's hell on earth," he groaned. "Does she know why you're going to Miami?"

"She knows we're going for a case, but doesn't know all the details yet.."

"That's probably for the best." He rubbed the stubble on his chin and narrowed his gaze. "But you're going to have to tell her at some point."

I nodded in agreement, and my stomach turned at the thought of doing it with anyone else. We'd taken on a new case a month ago and had tracked down a lead which led us to Miami. I figured I'd kill two birds with one stone and visit my parents while checking out the validity of the tip we had received at the same time.

But I had to convince Izzy to go with me. While she loved spending time with my parents, she hated Miami. I think it's because of the slick-tongued Latinas that lived near my parents. She didn't like to vie for hard-ass of the year with other females. Where we lived, no one rivaled Izzy.

"I know, Thomas. I'll tell her before we get there."

"I'm not exactly thrilled with the idea, but it's necessary that she get involved. She wouldn't want you to do this case with anyone else."

I would've left her home if I could, but the case required me to go to a **BDSM** club that was located only a few miles from my parents' house. I could've walked in there alone, but that would've opened me up to a slew of questions I didn't want to answer. Having my wife and submissive by my side made everything easier because I wouldn't be able to pull it off without someone I completely trusted.

"Angel okay with the kids staying over?" I asked, even though I already knew the answer.

I was sure Thomas had his ways of getting what he wanted out of his wife just like I did, but I didn't want to know the gory details.

"She's fine, and Nick's excited to have some company."

We'd taken Nick, Thomas and Angel's only kid, on plenty of weekends so they could get away and have some "private time." The poor kid never stopped smiling when he was around his cousins, and I always thought Thomas would have another so his kid wouldn't have to be alone.

"I can't thank you enough. I know your parents would take them again, but I think they'll have more fun playing with Nick and hanging with their favorite uncle."

"Don't butter me up. I'm taking the kids no matter what, so there's no need to lie to my face."

What I said was true. The kids loved every one of their uncles, but Thomas was their hands-down favorite. Maybe it was because he was a lot like me, and he and I had a special connection since we went through DEA training together and were thick as thieves.

Bear walked past the door and then backed up, glancing between Thomas and me. "Everything okay?"

"James is heading to Miami to follow that lead this weekend." Thomas turned, craning his neck to glance at Bear. "I'm going to need you to step up to second-in-command."

"I'll be whatever you need." Bear glided into the room, his chest a little more puffed out than usual, probably feeling pretty damn pleased about being asked to help take charge in my absence. "You sure you don't want me to handle the case instead?"

Thomas shook his head and laughed. "We're sure, man. Aunt Fran would fuckin' kill us."

Fran and Bear were a perfectly odd couple, if that made any sense. I never would've expected them to fall madly in love and become inseparable, but it happened. It shocked all of us, especially Morgan, Fran's son, but I'd never seen the old bastard happier.

"She's a cream puff," Bear replied with a straight face. "I can handle her."

"You'll be handling your balls for a really

long time if you mess with that woman," I told him because Fran made Izzy look like a kitten.

"Right." Bear laughed. "I'll help Thomas hold down the fort while you're gone. Morgan may be pissed, but…"

"He'll get over it," I told him. "He's too busy working the case with Sam right now to handle day-to-day operations for me. You'll be done with your current case this week, right?"

"I'm meeting with the client tomorrow, and then I'm free as a bird."

Bear had become an invaluable member of our team. When Joe mentioned that we should hire him, I'd thought he had gone completely off his rocker. Bear didn't have the cleanest background even though he'd been a family friend for many years. Now, I couldn't imagine him not being part of the ALFA crew. He always had our backs, no matter what crazy shit we found ourselves wrapped up in, and he typically saved the day because he didn't give a shit if he died as long as the rest of us got out safe.

"We'll meet later and go over the caseload and catch you up on everything," Thomas told him while I went back to checking my email.

"I'm your man," Bear said. "I'm going to go fuck around in my office for a bit before the afternoon meeting."

"Glad you keep yourself busy," I mumbled behind the screen.

"I'll pretend to check my email just like you," he shot back as he walked toward the doorway.

That was a lie. I never watched porn at work. Who needed porn when I had the real thing, my biggest fantasy, at home waiting for me?

"Fuck off." I waved my hand to the hallway, essentially dismissing him. "You sure you want him in charge?" I asked Thomas.

"He'll be fine."

"I picked him to take my place. Fucker better be. Now, let's talk about the case and how we're going to get this motherfucker."

We'd been brought in on a case where the FBI had hit a dead end. While they had to follow the law, we could skirt the edge and sometimes dip a toe over without many repercussions.

Since Thomas and I had both worked at the DEA and Sam had been a member of the FBI, we had contacts we often used in cases where we hit a roadblock, and they did the same when they needed a law or two broken.

They'd been tracking Matías Perez for three years and had no luck finding him before he had a chance to move on to his next destination. He was a known human trafficker, racking up more than ten thousand sales of individuals that he and his team had kidnapped all over the world in the last ten years.

Let that number sink in a bit…they've taken an average of one thousand people a year, at least the ones who made it to the sales floor, or three people per day. Each one, depending on condition, fetched between five thousand and ten thousand dollars each.

Ninety percent of their victims were women, often sold into sexual slavery in a country that wasn't their own, making the possibility of escape more difficult. Many times, they were sold to dingy brothels where they would be used and abused until their bodies gave out or they succumbed to disease. Then they'd be replaced by a new victim, and the cycle would repeat. Most women ended up in Asia, where the prostitution laws were lax or the government turned a blind eye because of payoffs and corruption.

Believe it or not, human trafficking is a huge problem and way more pervasive than most people think. Somewhere around four million people are trapped in sexual exploitation worldwide, but it's a fact that not many people like to talk about, especially politicians. It's messy and certainly not sexy or headline-grabbing like most garbage that's debated on cable news shows.

Matías was last spotted in Miami at the very same club I used to go to before I joined the DEA, where I learned what it meant to be a sexual dominant. My roots were there, but with Matías involved, I knew I couldn't let my guard down, even with the people I'd trusted before.

"How far are you willing to take this?" Thomas asked.

The club in Miami—Taboo—was our starting point, but I didn't have high hopes that it'd be the end of the case for us. He was probably on the move and his trail might have already gone cold, but I'd follow any lead I could until I either had nowhere else to go or caught the motherfucker.

"The question really is, how far do you

want me to take this? Your sister is going to need to be involved on some level."

He touched his fingertips together and placed them against his lips. His eyes roamed my face, pondering my statement. "We'll have to play it by ear. I don't want her involved if we can avoid it, and especially if she doesn't want to be."

"You know your sister doesn't do anything she doesn't want to do, and I'd never let anything happen to her."

Thomas cocked his head, lifting an eyebrow. "Best-laid plans, my friend. Look what happened with Rebel." He had a point.

"Yeah," I said, but I'd kill any asshole that tried to lay a hand on my wife. I'd broken bones for lesser offenses, and I'd have no problem snuffing out any scumbag that meant her any harm.

"See what you can find out in Miami, and then we'll decide how we want to move forward after that."

I nodded because I couldn't plan much

further ahead than that. Not with Izzy involved in what could very well end up being a complete shitshow. I had a feeling that the next week of my life would try not only my patience, but my sanity.

IZZY

"Seriously, James, I have to pee," I whined for the third time in ten minutes after he ignored me and told me to hold it. The man had the bladder of an elephant.

"We're almost to civilization. Can't you hold it a little longer?"

I gawked at him. Didn't he understand the struggles of a woman after birthing numerous children and our inability to hold it? Lord help me if I had to sneeze; there'd be no stopping the floodgates from opening.

"How much longer?" I wiggled in my

seat, moving back and forth, trying to seal up my girl bits and stop any leakage. "If you don't stop soon, I'm going to ruin this pretty little car of yours."

He floored the Challenger, putting every bit of the 707 horsepower to rocket us forward and closer to a bathroom quicker than if we'd had my Lexus RX. "Ten minutes. Tops."

I figured my comment about ruining his precious car would get his ass in gear and us out of the goddamn Everglades faster. Anywhere else in Florida and I would've run into the woods and taken care of business. But in the Everglades, there was no way in hell I was getting out of the car. I'd lived in Florida long enough to know what was in the woods and lurking in the water, waiting for a tasty morsel like me to put my pants around my ankles and bend over, unable to run and an easy mark.

We pulled into a tiny gas station, and before the car had even stopped, I was out the door and running to grab the key that I knew would be attached to the dumbest piece of hillbilly trash the owner could find. Like anyone would want to steal the key to the bathroom in the middle of Where-The-Fuck-Am-I, Florida.

I squeezed my thighs together, walking like I did as a kid after holding it too long at school and trying to make it into the house before I peed my pants. James watched me from the car with a smug grin, and I glared at him, flipping him the middle finger before unlocking the rusted door on the side of the building.

I hovered over the toilet that looked like it hadn't been cleaned in this decade and prayed that no tiny critters decided to make a surprise appearance. I hated being away from civilization and away from my slice of heaven that I called home. Being in the middle of Florida, where the alligators outnumbered the human population, creeped me out.

James owed me big for this. Not for spending time with his parents, but for sitting in a car for five hours listening to his music and having to pee for more hours than I cared to remember.

I didn't even bother to try to wash my hands. The faucets were covered in a brown slime, and I couldn't figure out if it was just dirt or… I didn't even want to think about it. I grabbed a wad of toilet paper and turned the handle, throwing it on the bathroom floor on the way out since there was no trash can. I was sure it would still be there on our way back in a few days if I had to make another pit stop.

"All better?" he asked as I opened the car door.

"No," I snarled. "Gimme a bottle of water and the sanitizer."

He scrunched up his face, knowing my issue with filth, but he didn't say another word as I poured the water over my hands and rubbed them together vigorously before dousing them in hand sanitizer and waving them around until they were moderately dry.

"Sorry about that." He revved the engine as I folded my body into the seat that was about four inches too low for the heels I decided to wear.

"It's fine. Are we almost to your parents'?"

"About thirty minutes away."

"I'm sure they're excited," I told him because I knew the last time we left, his mother cried the entire morning and probably kept crying until she didn't have another tear left to shed.

"My mom's been cooking all day."

The woman could give my mother a run for her money with the need to ply me with food. Her sole mission was to fatten me up and keep me healthy so I could raise her grandsons.

"I don't know why they don't move by us. The kids would love to have them around."

I'd even love to have his parents around. I loved them from the moment I met them, when his mother wrapped me in an embrace and called me her daughter. I knew that meant something special to her since she'd lost her daughter so tragically.

"We'll see. I think it would be good for them to be around the kids. I know they have to be lonely."

I glanced out the window, watching the rows of pine trees give way to buildings and finally civilization. Well, it was the suburbs of Miami and total insanity. There wasn't another soul for miles, and then...*wham!* Crazy-ass drivers and traffic out the ass.

"So why are we here?" I asked.

I'd been meaning to ask him since Friday night when he decided to torture me into submission. But it didn't matter, I was going with him anyway. I knew it was work-related because I heard him on the phone with Thomas, but he hadn't given me any details.

"Well." He glanced at me out of the corner of his eye. "We're here to get some leads."

I turned my body in the seat, wanting to

see his face when he answered. "And you needed me because…?"

In all the years he'd owned ALFA PI, not once had he asked me to come along on a case or help in any way. So, that left one of two things, either he needed a girl to get the answer, or it involved sex and he knew I'd castrate him if he even thought about taking someone else along for the ride.

"I need you on this one. I need a submissive."

I crossed my arms over my chest and narrowed my eyes. "A submissive or your submissive?" He had better answer that question the right way, or I'd flip my shit in a heartbeat.

"I need you and only you. I need the submissive who'll kneel at my feet and do as I say without a fight."

I cackled loudly because fight was my middle name. "Seriously? You want me to be that girl?"

"Sweetheart, you are that girl."

"It's been a long time since we've played, James."

Too long in fact. Last weekend had made the yearning I had for his domination grow after such a long drought of normal, only mildly kinky sex.

"It's not something you lose after a few months." He glanced in my direction with his piercing eyes. "And it's not something that can be faked with someone who isn't mine."

I never thought I'd like being called his. It made it seem like he was invoking territorial rights over me, but it always made my pussy throb and got my heart pumping.

"So we're going to a sex club in Miami?"

He nodded and gripped the steering wheel a little tighter, adjusting his body in the seat.

Fuck yeah. I was all in, baby. There was something about seeing James in the inner workings of a dungeon that got my pulse racing faster than the car we'd been sitting in.

The man had it.

He had the commanding spirit and the best qualities of the dirtiest master, with just the perfect amount of iron fist and soft love. There was no one else I'd ever let control me but him.

It wasn't like I'd gone looking for a sexual dominant, but I'd sure as hell found one.

We kept it in the bedroom, though, especially as the boys have grown older. The last thing I wanted them to think was that they could boss a woman around and get whatever they wanted. We kept our kink in the bedroom, or if I was lucky, at the club, and we remained completely fifty-fifty partners when we weren't getting our freak on.

"It's where I first honed my craft."

"So I get to meet the people who started you on your course of perversion?" I was almost giddy at the thought of meeting James's friends from back in the day.

Young James.

Hotter James.

And probably the world's biggest tool.

"Babe, you wouldn't love me without it."

He was right. I loved him for his strength. If he were weak, we'd never have worked. I'd be wearing the pants, and it would have gotten old quick. I loved control, but sometimes I wanted someone else to take the reins and handle shit so I could take a freaking break.

"It won't be easy for me to expose you to the group there."

Expose? I mulled the word over a bit, wondering if he wanted me to get naked or if just the very thought of introducing me to his Dom friends in Miami didn't sit well with him.

"I'll be fine," I reassured him, but I wasn't sure it did the trick.

"The group at our club is more social and a hell of a lot friendlier." I could feel his tension.

I reached across the console and placed my hand on his forearm. "I've dealt with pricks my whole life, James. I'm sure I can handle these guys."

"You will go in there fully clothed in an outfit that I choose and wearing my chain and collar so they know you're my property. There's nothing more to discuss."

I fingered the collar around my neck and remembered the day he gave it to me. That ceremony meant just as much as our wedding vows did in the church, but it had an entirely different meaning. Except the bit about obeying, but I doubted the church meant dropping to my knees and sucking him off when he commanded it.

"I'll be what you want, when you need it," I told him.

"We'll talk about it tonight before we go to the club," he said as we pulled into his parents' driveway. "Right now, we have to spend some time with my parents before we ditch them for a few hours." James turned to me, and my breath hitched because, well, my husband was hot as hell and he still yanked my chain. "Are you ready for this?"

"I was born ready," I told him with a big smile. "I'm a Gallo."

When James's mother opened the door and caught sight of us, she squealed with delight. Mrs. Caldo was the cutest damn woman, besides my mom, of course, and she always made me feel right at home. "Isabella, I've missed you." She pulled me into a bear hug, totally ignoring her son. Her hands squeezed my ass if she was assessing my squish factor. "You're too thin. We must fix this."

"Hey, Mama," James said behind me, and I was sure he felt a little left out of our love fest. "Can I get one of those?" Thankfully, he grabbed my shoulders, moving me out of her arms so he could finally hug her.

"My bebé, of course." She wrapped her arms around her son, looking so tiny against his wide frame.

There was something about seeing a man,

namely, my man, loving on his mother. She grabbed his face and peppered his cheeks with kisses before she moved on to his nose and forehead like he was a little kid. "I've missed you, Jimmy. It's been too long."

I giggled softly at the nickname. It was my go-to one when I wanted to piss him off, but his mother used it regularly, and he never corrected her. He'd probably get a shoe upside the head if he did, because Mama Caldo didn't play games. Sometimes she scared me, but I'd never admit it.

Mr. Caldo joined us outside and gave James a very firm and manly handshake before he turned his attention toward me. "Always so beautiful, Ms. Isabella." The way my name rolled off his tongue, I almost wished James had that accent.

Almost.

"It's so wonderful to see you again, Mr. Caldo," I nodded and reached my hand out, but he pulled me forward and smashed my chest against his.

"Papi, please."

"Papi," I said with a hint of a laugh.

Mr. Caldo's energy was contagious. I don't know if it was his Cuban heritage or just his zest for life, but I always loved being around him. James's mother was fun too, but she had the more serious personality like my mother. It must've been the Italian in her. But man, the Cuban and Italian mix in James made for a beast of a man.

James stood behind me with one eyebrow arched, watching his father get a little too handsy with me. "Pop, come on. She's mine. You got yours." James peeled his father's hands away from my body and tucked me into his side.

They talked about us like they owned us. James kind of owned me, even though I pretended he didn't. I wondered if it was the same way with his parents. The thought of it made me throw up a little in my mouth. I pushed the visual out of my mind, and I swallowed down my stomach acid.

"Thanks, Jimmy," I said, pretending he'd saved me from his father. But it was harmless, and Mrs. Caldo practically molested me every time I visited too. I just learned they were handsy people and accepted it.

I loved being at his parents' and being able to use that nickname without having to pay a penalty for it.

"Shall we?" Mr. Caldo said, motioning toward the house, which smelled like a little slice of heaven smack-dab in the middle of Miami.

James grabbed our suitcases while I followed his mother into the kitchen and took a seat at the island to watch her whip up another Cuban masterpiece.

James's mother may have been Italian by birth, but growing up in Miami and later marrying into the Caldo family, led to her embracing their Cuban culture wholeheartedly.

She slid a glass of wine in front of me. "Relax a little," she said. "I'm so glad you two came to visit. It's been too long, *hija*."

My insides warmed instantly as she called me daughter, and I sipped the wine slowly so I didn't get knocked on my ass and become useless to James later. "We've missed you too."

She stirred the beans, or *frijoles*, as she called them, slowly mixing them. "We've invited everyone over for dinner in a bit. I hope you don't mind."

I figured as much.

It was never just the four of us when we arrived. The entire extended Caldo family came out to gawk at their family member who married an Italian girl covered in tattoos and who didn't speak a lick of Spanish. Mrs. Caldo had been honorary Cuban for so long, everyone had forgotten she was really Italian like me.

My stomach growled when I caught a whiff of the *Arroz con Pollo*. "I don't mind at all as long as they all bring food." I'd quickly fallen in love with Cuban cuisine after becoming part of this family.

Moments later, the doorbell rang. It was

the start of the informal Caldo family re-union. The entire clan was just as handsy as his parents, but a hell of a lot of fun too.

"Izzy," Samara, his oldest cousin, squealed when she came running into the kitchen and wrapped her arms around me. "I've missed you, mama."

"Look at you," I said, turning around on the stool to give her a hug. *"Muy caliente."*

She backed away and pushed her chest out. "You like?" Her eyes dipped down to her new breasts, which were about three times the size of her old ones.

"I love," I said and gave her a nod of approval.

"Touch them." She bounced up and down, and her tits followed. "They feel so real."

I glanced around and shrugged, figuring why not. I'd touched hundreds of breasts after doing tattoos as long as I had. A tit is a tit, and I had a pair of my own too that I'd touched more times than I could count anyway.

They were nice for fake breasts. More than nice, actually.

Whoever did them did a killer job. I never would've guessed her rack wasn't real unless she'd told me. Bravo to the surgeon who'd pulled it off.

Samara and I could've been best friends if we lived closer. She was the type of girl I would've spent my time with and probably ended up under arrest with a time or two. She was a wild child and had absolutely no filter, but then again, none of the Caldos really did either.

I was in the process of fondling her when Mr. Caldo walked in and grabbed his chest. "Lord help me," he muttered and stumbled back a few steps.

"Oh, you old perv," Samara teased him and backed away from my hands.

Mr. Caldo slid next to Mama, clutching

her around the waist until she swatted him with her slotted spoon. "Hands off, *amor*."

"A man gets no love in this family," he said to the ceiling and raised his hands in the air as if he were defeated. "All the women touch, but Lord help a man."

"What are you complaining about, *anciano*?" Samara's husband, Che, asked as he walked into the room and threw his arm around her shoulder.

Being with the Caldos was no different than being at home with my family. They teased each other mercilessly, but it was backed by so much love that no one seemed to care what anyone said.

"Izzy was feeling my breasts when he walked in. So he's having a moment."

"Poor guy," Che said, but he brushed off the statement.

Okay.

Maybe they weren't entirely like the Gallos.

My dad always kept his hands to himself,

so this family was a wee bit different, but I was down with it. There was too much to love, and to each their own. It's not like he was feeling up his own relative, though it seemed that people who married into the family weren't always off-limits.

I didn't recall ever touching any of my brothers' wives' tits before. We hugged, sure. But that was as far as touching went except for maybe a poke of cleavage every once in a while. Here, I'd full on fondled Samara just like I was one of the family.

I shrugged it off and took a bigger sip of wine because my stomach hadn't stopped growling since the moment I walked in, and I was starving.

When driving through the Everglades, there wasn't a place to stop for a meal unless you wanted Willy's roadside shack that sold pieces of alligator which he'd kept stored in his cooler since the last hunting season. No fucking thank you. I didn't care how many times someone told me it tasted like chicken, that was a bullshit lie. The only thing that tasted like chicken was actually chicken. Alligator was a bit more rubbery and left a funk in my mouth that lasted too long and didn't wash away even with the strongest liquor.

"So, Izzy. How long are you two staying?" Che asked.

I was just about to answer when James sauntered into the room, rescuing me from the question. "Just a few days," he told Che.

"Damn. I was hoping we could hang out like old times." Che punched James's shoulder, barely moving him. "You look like you need to unwind a little."

"We might be free tomorrow," James said and wrapped his arm around my shoulder, mimicking Che with Samara.

"Yeah." I wanted to spend an evening with Samara and Che, my two most favorite people in his family, next to his parents, of course.

"We'll make time for you, cousin."

The doorbell rang again, and it sounded

like a stampede was happening in the foyer as the house filled with cousins, aunts and uncles, and other assorted family members.

I heard my name being called like I was a rock star about to take the stage. A girl like me could get used to this kind of love. Not that I was an attention whore, but it was good to feel welcomed by his family just as much as mine welcomed him.

The Caldos would always be my family. No matter what, they were my peeps just as much as they were James's.

I ate it up.

Soaked in their love, I reveled in it all until it was almost time to get down to business. I was stuffed to the gills with so much Cuban food I didn't know how I'd fit into the tiny outfit I knew James was going to make me wear. I wondered how the night would end.

To be honest, I looked forward to a little excitement with a dash of danger and couldn't wait to see what kind of trouble James and I would get into.

JAMES

"Remember your training and what I told you."

It had been so long since we'd been to a club that I wanted to cover all the rules and regulations with her before we entered. I couldn't have anything go wrong, or we'd be in a world of trouble.

The Doms here didn't play.

This was their life, and many of them lived the lifestyle 24/7. They'd probably have a coronary if they knew I gave my wife free rein over everything in her life and only played from time to time because of our kids.

I'd dressed Izzy before we left, taking my time to make sure her outfit and makeup were perfect. The slinky black miniskirt covered just enough of her body but gave a hint of ass without revealing too much to be acceptable at Taboo. The bustier she wore pushed her tits up nicely, but it hid her nipples well. The collar around her neck was freshly polished and glittered in the overhead lights of the parking lot as she walked next to me, staring at the ground.

I pushed her against the building and slid my hand up her thigh and under her skirt. "This is mine, and no one else will see it or touch it. Understand?" I murmured against her lips as I cupped her mound, pressing her back into the brick wall.

"Yes, Sir." She smiled and bit down on her lip, taunting me.

"I need you to listen tonight and pay attention to your surroundings for any information about Matías."

She nodded quickly and glanced down at the ground when she remembered her place, in case someone was watching. "Yes, Sir."

I'd be lying if I didn't admit that her calling me Sir made me hard as fucking granite. It was a high when a woman surrendered herself fully, but hearing the words come from Izzy's mouth meant more because she didn't easily hand over the reins of power.

"Good, girl." I yanked the chain, pulling her lips to mine and crashing my mouth over hers. I dipped my fingers inside her panties, finding her wet and ready.

She loved the power exchange. It turned her on and always had. I remembered the first time I ever took her to a club after we'd played at the house; she'd nearly lost her mind with lust. I'd never heard Izzy beg before, but I could still hear her sweet moans of pleasure to this day.

I rubbed my finger over her clit, pushing

her legs apart with my arm. "You want to come, doll?" I asked, but I wasn't going to give her what she wanted.

"Yes, Sir," she murmured against my lips and blew out a shaky breath as I plunged my fingers back inside of her.

My thumb grazed her clit, and her head tipped back, exposing her neck as I slid my fingers in and out of her without remorse. "You want me to fuck you?"

"Please," she begged as her pussy clamped down on my fingers, sucking them deeper.

She licked her lips, just as turned on by the idea as I was.

God, I missed this.

I missed us.

The way we used to be before shit got so complicated. I needed to change that and bring us back to our center, keeping our relationship rock-solid and worshiping my wife the way she deserved.

"Later, if you've been a good girl—" I smiled against her skin, licking a trail up to her ear "—I'll let you come." I pulled my hand from under her skirt, licking her wetness from my fingers and groaning as her taste exploded across my tongue. Tonight would test my restraint just as much as it would test her ability to submit.

Izzy didn't speak, just stared down at the ground with a hint of a smile on her lips. Wrapping the chain around my hand, I pulled her forward and toward the door. Her Jimmy Choo heels clicked against the cement with every step as she kept pace with me.

A small part of me regretted not being able to walk inside the club with my wife tucked under my arm. Although I was a Dom and there was no denying that, I was a man in love, and I was proud of the feisty little Italian spitfire I called mine.

The lobby of Taboo hadn't changed much, with its dark walls, faint sound of music, and the smell of sex. A man, one I knew well, stood behind the waist-high desk, flipping through a book. He looked up as soon as the door closed behind us.

"James?" Hagan narrowed his eyes. "Is that you?"

"It is," I said, stepping forward to shake his hand. "Good to see you, Hagan."

He looked exactly the same as he had the last time I saw him, almost twenty years ago. The only thing different was the amount of gray that framed his face and a few lines around his eyes.

"I didn't know you were coming back." He smiled, shaking my hand and almost breaking my fingers in his vise-like grip.

Hagan was one of the oldest and most established Masters at Taboo. He was also a sadistic motherfucker who liked to toy with his submissives and push them right up to their breaking point. But that never stopped them from lining up to feel the lash of his whip. They begged him for his brand of punishment, craving the pain he'd inflict. I'd never fucking understood it.

I could never be like him. I wasn't into the pain. I never got off on hurting others, even if the goal was to bring pleasure for all parties involved. Thank God pain wasn't Izzy's thing. I couldn't deal with hurting her even in the act of sex.

Deprivation was an entirely different matter.

That was my thing.

I enjoyed bringing her right to the edge of orgasm and ripping it away. Then doing it all over again. She liked it too. Sure, she whined and begged, but she always asked for more.

"Just for a night. I was in town and wanted to play with my girl, so I figured I'd come here."

His eyes drifted to Izzy, slowly raking up her body. "You always picked the lookers."

I cringed, because I knew Izzy was going to chew my ear off later for that comment. She'd grill me about the "lookers" and exactly how many there must have been for it to leave a lasting impression on Hagan.

"Hagan, she's my wife," I warned.

"Ah." His tongue clicked against the roof of his mouth. "I need to get a better look." The dirty old bastard rounded the desk and stopped next to me, clasping a hand on my shoulder while he looked down at Izzy. "May I?" he asked, needing permission to speak to her, and I nodded.

Izzy hadn't looked up, but the corner of her jaw ticked, probably still mulling over the comment about women I'd been with before I met her. Even when she was angry, she was still the most beautiful woman in the world, and I rethought my genius idea of bringing her here.

"It's nice to meet you, pet," Hagan said.

"Eyes, doll."

I knew he wanted to see her face. Hagan appreciated beauty as much as the next guy, but I knew what he'd see when he looked in her eyes. There was a fire that burned deep down in Izzy, and there was nothing she could do to hide it. It was that slow burn under the surface that made her so alluring to me when I met her…that and her smart mouth.

Izzy lifted her head and gazed up at Hagan, but she didn't speak.

"You have your hands full with this little one, don't you, James?" Hagan laughed softly and took a step forward, but he still maintained an acceptable distance for me not to put my body between them as a shield.

"That's what I love most about her."

Izzy chewed on the inside of her cheek and swallowed the words I knew she was dying to say. Probably something along the lines of "go fuck yourself" sat on the edge of her tongue, ready to put us in our place.

"Is she your only submissive, or do you have a more open arrangement?"

The moment I met Izzy, I knew I'd never share her. She had it…that quality that made me want to be a one-woman man, devoting my time, attention, and love to only her and no one else.

"I'm not into sharing this one, Hagan. I give her my full attention."

Hagan wasn't a one-woman type of guy. Although he had a devout submissive, he usually had a few slaves too. The man was more virile than most teenagers, wanting to conquer as much pussy as he could. The women never seemed to mind. He loved the openness of our world.

"I'd be the same with this one, James." Hagan turned his attention back to her. "It's entirely my pleasure to meet you, Mrs. Caldo." Hagan tipped his head and kept his hands to himself, following protocol within the walls of Taboo.

Izzy smiled, but she somehow remained silent.

"Sorry to cut this short, but…"

Hagan stepped back and away from the door. "I get it. Will you need a private room tonight, or will you be using the public areas only?"

The dirty bastard probably hoped I'd be

fucking my wife in public. I was sure we'd draw quite a crowd with her wails of ecstasy, killer tits, and the way she begged for my cock. So, that was a big hell no.

"A private room would be perfect."

"One doesn't open for another hour, but it's yours. I'll come find you when it's time and escort you. We don't normally let in non-members, but since I'm now part owner, I'll give you a pass. I know you're good to go. Do you need to store her clothes?"

"No, she'll remain dressed while in public." I shook his hand and made a mental note to see what I could get out of him about Matías. "Thanks for everything, Hagan." If Matías spent time here, then he had to be a regular and would have had to have filled out paperwork, including a background check, before he was able to gain entry.

"I'm always happy to help an old friend." Hagan walked around the desk and pushed a button on the wall, unlocking the main entrance to Taboo. I yanked Izzy's chain, pulling her forward as I opened the door.

"Have fun," Hagan called out as the music intensified, and the bass pounded against my chest twice as fast as my heart.

I glanced back as we walked through the narrow, barely lit hallway. Izzy stared down at the floor, twisting her hands together in front of her as she walked. I stopped before we entered the public room, pressing my fingertips to her chin and forcing her to look at me. "You're doing great. I promise I'll make this worth your while."

"You'd better rock my world, Jimmy," she whispered.

"Baby." I brought her mouth to mine. "I'm going to fuck you until you beg me to stop."

"Promises. Promises."

I slid my free hand up her back, fisting her hair roughly. "Be careful, little one, or I won't be so kind later."

Her eyes twinkled as my mouth crashed

down on hers, sealing her smartass comment before she could speak. When she melted into me, going almost slack in my arms, I knew she'd be quiet at least for a little while. When I pulled away, she was panting and breathless as I stared down at her.

My hand fell away, dropping back to my side as I took a step backward and appraised my wife. Bee-stung lips, flushed skin, and divinely decadent in her barely there outfit.

Her eyes cast downward, and I knew she was ready to enter the lion's den.

6

IZZY

I KNEELED AT JAMES'S SIDE, MAKING A LITTLE mental note to pay him back for this later. I assumed the position like the other women around me.

None of them moved, didn't even try to make eye contact, and seemed almost invisible as they clung to their Masters. James had warned me about this crowd. That they took the D/s relationship very seriously, and most of them had slaves and not submissives. Back home, at our club, it was more relaxed and playful, but here…not so much.

I, on the other hand, didn't stare at the ground like the other women. James talked with his old friends, barely noticing me.

While keeping my head slightly downcast, I used the opportunity to take in as much of my surroundings as I could from under my eyelashes without getting reprimanded.

How could I gather anything unless I took a little peek, right?

My eyes drifted to a stage where a small crowd gathered, watching a woman being flogged. She seemed to orgasm with every lash. Lucky cunt. Not that I wanted to get my ass beat, but anything that would bring me that much pleasure, I'd be all in and begging for more. Her ass was beet red as sweat glistened on her skin in the overhead lighting.

The man turned, speaking to the crowd, but I couldn't make out the words over the music wafting through the open space. He faced her again, lashing her as she jolted with a scream. But it wasn't one of horror or pain. It was pure pleasure and turned into a moan that I could hear loud and clear even over the beat of the song playing.

I slid my hand up James's pant leg, gripping the back of his calf, turned on by what I saw, but also scared to death. His fingers tangled in my hair as he stroked my scalp, maybe feeling some of my anxiety or lust.

My emotions were always scattered in places like this. It was hard to rationalize what coursed through my system when I watched someone else getting off while figuring what they were enduring was anything but pleasant. Yet it was. The noises she emitted made it impossible for me to think any differently.

"Are you still into sharing?" Anders asked James.

The thought of being with any of these guys had my head spinning—and not from excitement. I didn't want them, not when I already had the only man I wanted. But I knew, back in the day, he used to be into that type of thing. He told me when he'd become a member at Taboo, he wasn't above sharing a sub with another Master recreationally, or if that was what the scene called for and the sub needed it.

Whatever the fuck that meant. At no time had I been strapped to our bed thinking, man, I'd love some pussy grinding on my face. Hell, I never even thought I could go for an extra cock to fill some empty part of my body while James banged the ever-living fuck out of me. Maybe that was where I was different. I was a one-man woman. Even if we hadn't been married, I wasn't sharing him. Ever.

From the moment he told me about his kink, I made it crystal fucking clear to James that I wasn't a toy to be passed around to his friends. He said nothing like that would ever happen because he didn't share what was his anymore. Fucker better have said that, or I would've been out the door in a heartbeat.

"No, Anders. I've never shared her, nor do I ever plan to either." He gripped my hair and pulled my head back so I was forced to look him in the eyes. "This one is only for me."

I couldn't stop the small smile from spreading across my face. "Isn't that right, doll?"

"Yes, Master," I said, kind of digging the dirtiness of the words and feeling totally in tune with our current surroundings. Plus, I wanted to show my husband that I could follow directions…at least sometimes.

I'd be lying if I didn't admit it made my entire body tingle when he spoke those words. The man still lit my torch after all these years. I never would've believed that after more than ten years of marriage we'd still be going strong and that I wouldn't have kicked his bossy ass to the curb. But I'd honestly never been happier in my life.

"Shame," Anders said as James released my hair and I bowed my head again. "You did well for yourself."

I rolled my eyes, and thankfully, no one could see since I stared down at the ground like the other women around me. "Fucker," I muttered softly enough that I knew no one could hear me.

Anders reached down and fondled the breasts of the woman kneeling at his feet. "I would've swapped. Cat loves to play with new partners." His fingertips wrapped around her nipples and twisted until she shifted on her knees and whimpered. "It could've been fun to watch the two beauties together."

Yeah.

No.

Pussy had never been my thing.

I'd always been a dick girl.

Why the fuck would I want to "play" with another woman when I had the same parts and they didn't impress me one bit. There wasn't anything better than a hard cock, filling me until I couldn't breathe. I didn't need a girl sticking her tiny little fingers in me or licking my clit. There was nothing I wanted more than a hard dick or the thick fingers of a man working in and out of my pussy while the stubble of his hair rubbed against my thighs as he ate me like a man obsessed with pussy.

"Aria," Rider said, glancing down at his sub. "Would you like to play with Cat? She's lonely."

Rider was… I didn't even know how to explain the man other than slightly scary. He was bigger than James, with long black hair that fell just below his shoulders. His eyes were the blackest I'd ever seen, where the iris and pupil ran together, and I couldn't tell where one stopped and the other began. His facial hair was a mix of black and gray, covering his lips almost completely. There was something about him that sent a shiver down my spine when he spoke.

Out of the corner of my eye, I saw Aria raise her head and look into Rider's eyes and say, "Yes, Master."

Well, all righty, then.

I guess he didn't force her since he'd asked. But I wondered how many of the women around me ever voiced their disapproval? I knew that, in the lifestyle, no Master was supposed to force any sub to do anything. The relationship was about trust most of all, but it still gave me pause. Because let's face it, in all walks of life there are assholes, and that meant that even a percentage of Masters are dickheads too.

How many of the woman, and male slaves, for that matter, were as vocal and feisty as I was with James? Probably not very many. I knew when I broke into my "I'm going to be a cunt today because fuck it...I want to" mode that James would pay me back with some cock and a spanking. Both things I loved. So it was a win-win for me. I think James just wanted to fuck the asshole attitude right out of me, and it always seemed to work.

Neither Aria nor Cat moved, waiting for their orders and permission like any good sub would under the circumstances. Rider stood first, moving away from the couch he and Anders sat on.

"Move onto the couch and lie down," Rider told Aria, pulling her to her feet. "I want to watch Cat eat that beautiful, sweet pussy. No coming unless I say. Understand, li'l one?"

Men…such assholes.

That was bullshit. Seriously.

Like, who can hold off an orgasm when someone's sucking on your clit and ramming their fingers in your cunt? I mean, let's get real. Ain't nobody got that ability. Nobody. I don't care if you've done enough Kegels to make your twat the most muscular and controlled pussy in the world…you can't stop from coming when someone's latched on to your body like they're drinking the best damn milk shake in the world, sucking and slurping the most sensitive part of your body.

Anders followed Rider to a set of empty chairs on the side of James as Cat and Aria crawled onto the couch. Looked like we were going to get an up close and personal show while the guys chitchatted.

I hadn't gotten a good look at either of the women since they'd had their heads down since the moment I joined them. But I could see them fully now…every inch of their naked bodies. They were stunning.

Aria lay down, pulling her body so her ass was on the cushions, and Cat nestled between Aria's legs while kneeling on the washable vinyl couch.

Thank God for fake leather. Times like these made me grateful to be on the floor and not sitting on something that'd probably had more come on it than any street-corner hooker.

"Cat," Anders said as she started to move her face closer to Aria's bare pussy. "Don't stop until I tell you to."

Cat nodded with a small smirk before pushing Aria's legs farther apart and burying her face. Aria let out a loud moan, pushing her back deeper into the cushions and her pussy into Cat's face.

James shifted in his chair, and I dug my

fingernails into his skin, reminding him I was still there. It was like watching a porno but having it close enough that you could almost smell the arousal coming off the two women in waves.

I was a little bit jealous, if I were being completely honest. I knew James was turned on by what was happening right in front of us. I mean, he was a man. There was no way he could stop himself from being horny from it, any more than Aria could control her orgasm. I had to remind myself of that repeatedly as I sat there with the girl-on-girl action happening only a few feet away while the guys talked.

After they ogled the women on the couch for five minutes, Rider finally asked the one question I'd been waiting for. "What brings you back to Taboo, James?"

7

JAMES

I PAUSED FOR A MOMENT AND GLANCED DOWN at Izzy. She clung to my leg, eyeing the girls and the stage area, even though she was pretending to stare at the ground. She never could follow orders, but I knew Anders and Rider weren't paying attention to her anyway. If I hadn't known Izzy better, I would've thought she was staring at the ground too. But she's Izzy and never has followed directions. It was why we had so much fun together.

There were very few people that I trusted. The guys at ALFA PI and anyone I called family I trusted with my life and Izzy's too. But at Taboo, with so many new faces and over a decade since I'd stepped foot through the doors, I wasn't sure who still had my back except for the two men who sat next to me and maybe Hagan. They'd mentored me from the moment I became an official member at Taboo and never fucked over another person as far as I remembered.

Rider had an iffy past, much like Bear, but I knew he was rock-solid and trustworthy. I had Thomas run a criminal search on him before I arrived, just to be sure he was still on the up-and-up. If someone at Taboo had been pulling some shit, I assumed he'd know because trouble tended to follow him.

Anders was a lawyer by trade and seemed to know everyone at the club, taking on more than a few of them as clients in the past. He and I kept in touch over the years, getting together outside of the club for a beer anytime I made it back to Miami.

Even though we were friends, I wasn't

sure they'd willingly hand over information about another member. It wasn't something that was typically done, no matter how much they may have disliked the person. What happened at Taboo stayed in Taboo, and no one wanted to get into each other's business. But since I knew these men, and Matías was such a motherfucker, I hoped they'd help.

"I'm here looking for information on someone."

This wasn't the sort of place I was used to conducting business. Sex clubs were where I went to have fun and unwind, not question someone about the whereabouts of a criminal. But here we were, sitting in front of two girls going at it with Izzy kneeling at my leg as I started the questions.

"We were told that he spent time at Taboo, and I figured I'd come here to see if I could get any leads."

Anders and Rider glanced at each other, but Rider spoke first. "If you're looking for him, then he's bad news. You know we vet every member very carefully."

"What's his name?" Anders asked, glancing at Aria and Cat.

They were going at it, and struggling, suffering Aria was biting her lip and slithering around the couch, trying to avoid Cat's lips.

Poor girl. None of us was even paying attention to them anymore, and I knew Rider wasn't going to give Aria permission to come anytime soon.

"Matías."

Anders rubbed his chin and furrowed his brow as he pondered the name. "I don't remember a Matías. Was he here lately?"

"Yeah. About a month back."

Rider leaned back in his chair and crossed his arms, his expression matching Anders's. "You got a picture of him? Because the name doesn't ring a bell."

I figured Matías, being high-profile and one of the top wanted men in the country, wouldn't use his real name. But then again, there were stupid criminals everywhere…just not Matías. The man had evaded some of the best minds in the FBI, and they'd only caught a whiff of him after he'd already vanished.

I reached into my pocket before unlocking my phone and pulling up a photo of him. I handed it off to Anders, and Rider leaned in to take a look.

"Ahh," Rider said and nodded. "I remember this asshole."

"Me too. Complete dick." Anders handed the phone back to me and shook his head. "He left because Hagan and I threw his ass out. What's he wanted for?"

"Human trafficking." In our community, that was a hard limit, and I didn't want their subs to overhear.

Anders and Rider rocked back in their chairs like I'd punched them in the gut. It was something that could never be forgiven. Everyone in this club was here under their own free will to have fun and live out their every fantasy.

"Son of a bitch," Anders muttered and scrubbed his hand down his face. "He was so rough with a few of the girls too."

"Didn't…what's her name disappear?" Rider turned toward Anders and snapped his fingers.

"Victoria?" Anders answered quickly. "She did."

"You think he had something to do with it?" Rider asked.

"Come on. Girls stop coming to the club all the time. It's probably nothing," Anders told Rider.

"I don't know, but I'll find out," I told them, adding a visit to Victoria's to my agenda before we headed back to the other coast.

If she was truly missing, Matías would be my number one suspect. "When did she stop coming around?"

"A few days ago," Rider replied.

"No cops came by?"

"None." Anders shook his head quickly.

"That's a good sign," I told them.

"We'll see what else we can find out and let you know." Anders stood up and stretched. "I think I should put her out of her misery."

Rider laughed, smacking his leg, and followed Anders toward the ladies. "Ask Hagan on your way out. He handles all applications and might have something useful."

"Will do." I tipped my head and looked down at Izzy.

Anders grabbed Cat by the hair, pulling her lips off Aria. "That's enough, girl. I have something better for you to fill your mouth with." She climbed off the couch gracefully, still held by the hair, and followed him as he walked her toward the private room.

Rider stared down at Aria, still lying there with her legs wide open and gasping for air. "Did you come, li'l one?"

She licked her lips with her eyes glazed over as she gazed up at him. "No, Master."

"Up you go. Let's get you taken care of."

Rider had a devilish smirk on his face as he helped Aria off the couch.

"They're hard-core," Izzy whispered.

She was right. I used to be the same way, but time and Izzy changed me. It wasn't a bad thing. Hell, I still tried to control her to this day. It was my nature. I was made that way.

"I know, doll. It's a good thing you're with me," I told her, touching her chin and pulling her lips toward mine as I bent over. "It's a good thing you have me."

She laughed right in my face. "Babe, let's be honest…it's a good thing you have me."

Thankfully, no one was around to see her display of arrogance. "Mind your place," I reminded her, sealing my lips over hers and swallowing what I assumed was going to be another smartass comment.

They'd take my man card if they knew half the shit I'd put up with over the years from Izzy. But I loved the woman, and I'd do anything to keep her happy… Well, almost anything. She pushed my buttons as much as I pushed hers.

Her hand slid up my legs and came to a rest against my stiff cock. "You turned on by that?" she murmured against my lips. "By the girls?"

"I'm turned on by only one thing…" I wrapped my fingers around her chin and held her gaze. "By my wife."

She tilted her head and gazed up at me. "Good answer."

I moved quickly, wrapping my arms around Izzy's waist and hoisting her over my shoulder as I stood. She grunted and wiggled against me until I swatted her ass hard enough that she yelped and finally stilled. "I think it's time for me to remind you who owns you."

"I'll be good," she said, but I knew Izzy didn't understand the meaning of that word.

The woman would fight me if I told her the sky was blue, just because she wanted to be a thorn in my side and she loved to argue about everything.

I stalked toward the private rooms with Izzy over my shoulder and my hand over her backside, making sure no one got a peek of her beautiful ass along the way.

Even at our club back home, I never let her be naked in front of anyone. We mainly went there because I didn't want to risk having a room set up at home and the kids wandering in there and catching a glimpse of all the contraptions. I wouldn't even know where to begin explaining any of it to them, and I knew Izzy would be at a loss too.

Hagan stood near the hallway with a big grin. "Your room is ready. Third one on the right," he said.

"Is it the same as it was before?"

He nodded, and I kept walking because I had a feisty woman who needed a lesson and a raging hard-on that needed a hole... I wasn't picky either. Depending on her fight, I'd use them all if she wasn't careful.

When I kicked the door closed, Izzy lurched her head up and gasped. "I'll be good," she said, squirming out of my arms. "Come on."

When Hagan had confirmed that the room hadn't changed, I'd almost skipped down the hallway, filled with such happiness. This was the torture room, looking every bit like a medieval dungeon, and it usually scared the hell out of the subs. I had no plans to torture my wife, but it was funny as hell to watch her backtrack her smartass comments. But there were a few things in the room that were useful.

She slid down my body until her feet touched the floor. She reached up, caressing my face with her slender fingers and blinking slowly, feigning innocence. "Make love to me," she whispered.

Oh, she was good. But her bullshit good-girl act wasn't enough to get me off track.

"Doll," I said, rubbing her shoulders and backing her up toward the punishment bench.

"I'm going to show you just how much I love you."

"Yeah?" she asked with a smile, but it quickly faded when she glanced over her shoulder and saw exactly what I was moving her toward. "You want me on that?"

"What did you make me promise?"

She licked her lips, and her eyes flashed with hunger. "You said you'd fuck me until I begged you to stop."

I nodded and smiled as my cock hardened even more. "Now get undressed, climb up there, and assume the position."

If I could pick one piece of equipment to put in our house, it would be a punishment bench. It sounded so much more sinister than it really was, at least in my hands. It was a metal, bench-like structure that had an adjustable horizontal bar for the sub's stomach to comfortably rest upon as their ass was up and head down. It left every hole open and easily accessible for their partner to do with as he wished. It was perfect, and the cuffs for the wrists and ankles made the entire package complete.

"You promise you're going to be nice?" She quirked an eyebrow at me, knowing she'd been naughty.

"Cross my heart."

"You putting that—" Her eyes dipped down as I started to undress and my cock sprang free from my pants "—in my ass?"

"Don't test my patience," I warned her with a stern look.

"This place better have a lot of lube," she muttered as she climbed out of her skirt and panties before tossing them onto the bench near the doorway.

She hadn't stopped squabbling since I brought her in here, and she knew that it just meant more time. I swear she did it on purpose to get a rise out of me. Sometimes she'd tell me that she liked normal, everyday lovemaking, but I knew she was lying. Izzy couldn't verbally admit she liked to be dominated because it would've made her appear weak, but the wetness between her legs told me the truth.

I closed the space between us and stuck my hand between her legs. "You're wet, doll." She squeezed her eyes shut, shivering against my hand. "You want this more than you're willing to admit. Save your breath. Get up there, and show me that pussy."

When I finished speaking, her eyes opened, but they were different. The fight was gone, replaced by lust and need. I knew my wife better than I knew anyone in the world, and she was a horny beast.

I watched with my arms crossed and my cock jumping with anticipation as she slowly finished undressing before climbing onto the bench. When she finally found a comfortable spot for her forearms and legs on the padded spots, she stilled.

I should've strapped her in right away, but I couldn't resist touching her before I did. I moved behind her, taking in the sight of her beautiful pussy and tight little ass spread out before me. Placing my hands on her cheeks, I kneaded them softly.

"You want my cock?" I asked, letting my thumbs almost touch her pussy.

"Yes," she said, breathy and wanton.

"You want me to fuck this beautiful cunt?"

Her bottom moved as if she were chasing my fingers and wanting more than I offered. "Yes, Sir."

I slid my hands between her legs, running my fingertips over her clit before dragging them back through her wetness and pressing two into her warmth. Her hands wrapped around the armrests, and her head fell forward with a sigh.

"You love when I fuck your greedy pussy, don't you?"

She nodded, not able to form words as I stroked her G-spot. I raised my hand, letting it come down hard on her round ass, with the fingers of my other hand still buried deep inside her.

"Speak," I reminded her. "I need your words, doll."

"Fucker," she muttered, but her pussy clenched against me, and I knew I had her, that she wanted this just as much as I did.

"Your disobedience calls for the restraints and a blindfold."

God. Fucking with Izzy's head was such a high. I think it was mostly because of her smart mouth that it turned me on so much. Stunning her to silence was such a victory and an achievement so major that I should get a medal because it was damn near impossible sometimes.

"You wouldn't," she dared me, turning her head so she could see my face.

"I will, and if you're not good, I'll get the ball gag too." Her eyes widened as she gritted her teeth to swallow down the words she so badly wanted to say.

She bowed her head, relaxing against the stomach bar, and waited for me to strap her down. I worked quickly, excitement coursing through my veins with every click of the lock.

Tonight, I was going to use my wife as my own personal fuck toy and enjoy every goddamn second of it.

8

IZZY

I COULD BARELY MOVE WHEN I FINALLY opened my eyes. I lay there, groaning through the pain as I untangled myself from James's body and collapsed onto my back.

I didn't even know what time we finally made it back to his parents' house because I passed out in the car. My legs barely functioned after being strapped to that fucking bench for hours while James forced me to orgasm.

Forced was the wrong word.

I wanted them…every single fucking one

of them too. *But, whoa.* It had been years since James fucked me like that. He used me, and I'd do it all again in a heartbeat.

I thought once the kids were older that it would be easier to get our kink on, but it seemed the problems had grown with them, along with the time span between our "workouts."

At least, that's what we told the boys we were doing when we left the house dressed in our tracksuits to hide our real clothes underneath and a duffel bag filled with so many sex toys I couldn't even carry the damn thing.

"Izzy," James's mother said, tapping lightly on the door. "Are you awake?"

James stretched, hogging the bed and nearly knocking me off the edge with his long, thick limbs. "Yeah, Mama."

"Can I come in?" she asked.

"One second," I yelled out, yanking the sheets and comforter over our naked bodies and his delicious morning wood.

James glanced at me with a soft, sweet smile. "Morning, sweetheart."

"Hey, tiger." I winked, feeling playful and achy.

Although I hated the drive and leaving my tiny bubble, the weekend had turned out amazing so far with the food, family, and fucking. They were the three most important Fs in life and the very things I couldn't live without.

The door creaked open, and his mother padded into the room so quietly I wouldn't have heard her if she hadn't knocked. She was so damn cute like my ma, only a little rounder and loved wearing muumuus, which I'd never believed people actually wore in real life until I met her. Her brown hair with gray highlights was pulled back in a bunch and held in place with a yellow pencil.

"Are you hungry?" she asked and looked toward the wall and not directly at us.

"We're covered." James laughed and stretched again at my side.

She glanced our way with a small smile. "I figured you two were hungry, so I made a big lunch. I didn't want everything to get cold."

Lunch? The only thing I needed was coffee and two aspirin to ease the ache in my muscles. I couldn't deal with a spicy four-course meal when I was barely even awake and functioning.

"We'll be out in a few minutes, Mama. Let us wake up a little."

She blushed as her eyes scanned over us, probably realizing we were naked. She took three slow steps backward. "I hope I didn't…" she started to say, but her voice trailed off.

"No," James said quickly as I giggled.

"Uh," she muttered and stepped out into the hallway and pulled the door with her. Before it closed, she peeked inside and smiled. "I could use another grandbaby." The door closed quickly, and she disappeared before either one of us could reply.

James rolled on top of me, grinding his dick into me. "Wanna give it a shot?"

I stared at him, not amused by the idea. "Are you kidding me?"

His eyebrows drew together as he gazed down at me, his body pressed against mine. "I never kid about fuckin', doll."

"I'm all about the dick, but not another baby."

He tilted his head up, and his eyes darted around the room as if he was thinking about it. He'd better not be. "Just messin' with your head. Our babies are more than I ever wanted. I'd rather have some alone time with my wife and my favorite part of her body." He smirked.

"Not to be a party pooper, but I'm hungry and a little sore from last night."

That comment made his smirk grow into the biggest damn I'm-so-proud-of-myself-for-making-you-ache smile. "We better feed you. I wanted to go back to the club tonight. You game?" He arched an eyebrow.

I would've said no, but my pussy contracted at the thought of that damn bench and all the dirty shit he did with me. I couldn't help but say, "Fuck yeah." Plus, I was hoping I'd find out more about the old James…the one before I ruined him forever.

He nuzzled his face into my neck, bumping my very sore middle with his rock-hard dick. "Missin' my cock already, baby?"

"Always." I smiled.

I'd learned it was easier to puff up his ego than to tell him what I was actually feeling. At least at times when he thought he was the man, with his mighty pecker that held the secrets to whatever bullshit guys told themselves. They were insecure creatures who seemed to need constant reassurance from the moment they were born. So, I rolled with it. Telling him a white lie saved me time and a whole lot of hassle.

"I have plans for you tonight."

Now, that had my attention. "Do I get to be the Master tonight?"

James howled, rolling onto his back and taking me with him. His fingertips dug into my hips as he slid my body against his cock, sending a shiver down my spine. "Baby, you think you want control, but I own your body."

"Let's not kid ourselves, sweetheart. My pussy rules you," I told him with a sinister laugh.

Because, in all reality, he might have thought he held the reins, but my pussy controlled his everything. Right down to the way he thought and his day-to-day actions.

If we were being completely honest, we'd all agree that pussy made the world go round.

Men weren't motivated to become wildly successful and filthy rich just for shits and giggles. Wealth and power usually turned the ugliest man into a pussy king, obtaining gold-digging beauty queens who previously would've been out of his league.

Even their most basic actions were based on pussy. They knew if they did one thing, they'd be paid in all the sweet cunt they could handle. But if they did the other, they were going to have blue balls until they earned their way back to the motherland. See, I knew how the world worked. I knew James was motivated by what was between my legs. I was okay with it. I was more than okay; I accepted it and used it to my advantage.

After I climbed off James and made myself presentable, we sat around the table with his parents and feasted on so many Cuban goodies I was pretty sure he'd have to roll me into Taboo tonight. I leaned back in my chair, rubbing my stomach and lost in a blissful food coma.

Mr. Caldo folded his newspaper carefully and set it next to his plate. "It's so nice to have you kids here. I wished you lived closer."

"When are you two going to move by us?" James asked his father.

"Ask your mother." He rolled his eyes and raked his fingers through his salt-and-pepper hair. "She's the boss."

His mother grabbed a stack of plates and

headed toward the sink. "We've been discussing it. I love everyone around here, but I need to spend time with my grandchildren before they get too old."

"You do, Mama. You could spend time with them whenever you want."

That was code for we were going to drop them off for a weekend so we could fuck like bunnies without the kids knocking on the door and interrupting our fun. Sometimes I felt guilty about it, but once the house was whisper-quiet, the guilt passed quickly. It would be nice to have someone else to leave them with for a weekend, besides my parents. Anyway, the kids loved being away from us because my parents tended to go overboard with them and spoil them rotten. It was amazing my boys weren't complete assholes because of them.

"Maybe we'll come visit and look at some places," Mr. Caldo said. "We could use a little trip, Rose."

She leaned against the counter, wiping her

hands on a towel and smiling. "Whatever you want, Evaristo."

Shit was serious when they used their full names. I prayed this conversation wasn't for show. I would love to have his parents closer, not just so we could bang like bunnies, but so the boys could really get to know his parents and more about his Cuban heritage. They have the Italian bossy male thing down pat. Someday, their wives will be telling me how much I ruined them, and I'll be proud.

"Darling." Mr. Caldo rose to his feet, almost gliding across the floor to embrace his wife. "You know it's whatever you want." He nuzzled her neck, rubbing his whiskers against her skin. "Isn't that right, Mama?"

She smacked him on the shoulder and laughed.

Another perfect example that girl power ran the world. We just let the men think they were in charge. It was all a grand illusion that kept the world turning.

If men realized we held the power, there

would be an uprising until they got horny enough to cave.

They all did in the end.

Six hours later, we walked into Taboo for another night of sextivities. I spent the afternoon in the hot tub, soaking my ass and gearing up for another evening of being used by James. I wanted nothing to get in our way before we headed back to the west coast and picked up the boys at Thomas's.

James dressed me again, but thankfully, the man had good taste. Some of the women walking into Taboo had on the tackiest latex outfits that I wouldn't be caught dead in, even if the Master holding my chain had an eighteen-inch pecker and made me orgasm from a single touch. I didn't want to look like a complete wank in public even if it was at a sex club. Tonight, he'd dressed me in a dark turquoise bustier, with a black skirt that barely covered my ass and my favorite black Lady Peep Louboutins. Thank God he knew the difference between vixen sexy and trashy whore.

I picked at the edge of my skirt, trying to pull it down a little because Hagan's office was like a meat locker. But the material wasn't forgiving and wouldn't budge.

Hagan sat across from us, flipping through a filing cabinet filled with past member's applications. "I remember that bastard. He seemed okay, but he was one of the nastiest pricks we've had in here. I had to toss him out. I still can't believe I fucked up."

James had asked him about Matías, showing him a photo, and shared the details of the investigation. Hagan went off the rails, slamming his hands down on the desk and muttering profanities about how he'd let a criminal slimeball into the club.

"It happens, Hagan. Don't be so hard on yourself," James told him as I sat next to him, glancing around the office and staying relatively silent. "Guys like him know how to fly under the radar just long enough to get what they want. If the FBI can't catch him, why would you?"

Hagan let out a huff as he pulled out the folder for Kent Wilken, the alias Matías had used when applying at Taboo. Even with a thorough background check, nothing sent up a red flag, so he was permitted a trial membership, which was then revoked due to his piss-poor behavior.

Hagan slid the folder across the desk before leaning back in the metal chair, rocking back and forth with his lips twisted. The guy was intense and a little bit scary, but some people would probably say the same thing about James just by looking at him.

A photo on a shelf to my right caught my eye. It was of a group of men with oversized cigars hanging from their lips as they held up a gator they must've caught during alligator hunting season years ago. The man on the far left looked like my Jimmy, only twenty years younger and way tanner. Hagan was in the photo too—younger, handsome, and with the same intense stare he still had.

But I kept staring at James. He looked so happy, carefree, and hot as fuck. He was still mouth-watering, but damn it if he wasn't drop-dead gorgeous in his early twenties. I would've been all over that. Wait. I was, not too many years after that photo was taken. The rest was history. I imagined he had quite the following at Taboo too before he joined the DEA and eventually ended up in my bed.

James flipped through the folder on Kent aka Matías. When my leg started to shake, he placed his hand on my knee with a light squeeze. I dragged my eyes away from the photo and glanced at him with a smirk. Some women might be jealous when they thought about their husband's past, but I wasn't. I was proud he was mine, and above all, he slipped a ring on my finger and not anyone else's.

"Can you make a copy of everything in

here for me?" James asked, closing the folder and placing it on the desk in front of us.

Hagan grabbed the folder and nodded. "Anything you need, James. You know that."

"I'll pick it up on my way out."

Hagan smirked, raising an eyebrow. "Staying for a little while?"

"We had such a great time last night, I thought I'd treat my wife to another night." James peered over at me and winked.

My face heated with embarrassment, but it quickly vanished when a dull, steady ache settled between my legs at the memory of last night. If James was giving, I was all about receiving.

"Same room?"

"What's open?" James slid his hand up my thigh and settled his fingertips just under the hem of my skirt. The ache turned into a deep, needy throb.

"Paradise, Punishment, or Pain."

"Hmmm," James muttered, his eyes sliding to me as I chewed on my bottom lip.

Fuck, I had punishment last night, and that was kick-ass. I'd take anything they had to offer because one thing I knew about my husband, he was going to do me so good that I'd be walking funny tomorrow.

A slow smile spread across James's face as he looked over at a waiting Hagan. "Paradise."

"Ahh." Hagan chuckled. "My favorite."

Everyone else was smiling, so I did too. Fuck yeah. Bring on paradise, baby.

"It'll be open in an hour," Hagan told us, typing James's name into the schedule. "Until then, there's a demonstration on whips in the main room that your li'l one might enjoy."

Um, nope.

I was not a whip girl.

Never been one and never would be. Even if that shit was hot last night. The girl who got her back almost branded by the soft leather looked like she dug it, and therefore, it was sexy. But in no way, shape, or form was James ever to use a whip on me. The man would soon find his balls missing if he even tried.

Now, spanking… That was an entirely different story. I relished the sting of his hand against my ass, especially when his dick was buried so deep inside me that I could barely breathe. That was hot, and I did as much bad shit as I could just so James would smack my ass.

Sometimes a girl had to do what a girl had to do to get her rocks off. Plus, messing with James's head was fun, and the spanking was the bonus.

James stood and yanked the chain attached to my collar. I was too lost in thought about the girl being whipped and all the ways I'd make James pay if he did the same thing to me. I scrambled to my feet, ready to head to paradise, but not before doing everything I could to earn a few spankings tonight.

9

JAMES

I KNEW IZZY HAD THE WRONG IDEA ABOUT THE pleasure room as soon as the words came out of Hagan's mouth. It wasn't about her pleasure, but mine. She still hadn't realized it when I locked her hands in the overhead cuffs that hung down from the ceiling because she was practically buzzing with anticipation.

"You've been a bad girl, Izzy," I told her as I closed the clasp on the ankle restraints that were bolted to the floor. "A very bad girl."

"I'm sorry," she whispered, but she wasn't.

She never was. "I think you should spank me." She licked her lips, staring down at me with hooded eyes.

I looked back down at her foot, grabbing her other ankle to hide my smile. This woman. She was maddening and insatiable and totally mine. While we'd waited for the room, she'd made sure to break more than a few small rules. More than once, she didn't address me properly and looked me in the eyes when I didn't tell her to. Plus, she made sure to do it in front of other people. She wanted the spanking so badly, but then again, I wanted to give it to her too.

I dragged my fingertips across her bare ass and pressed my lips to her neck. "Do you deserve a spanking?"

Her head fell back, fully exposing her neck as it rested on my shoulder. "Yes, Master."

"Do you want a spanking?" I smiled against her skin, knowing damn well she wanted it and was about to lie.

"No, Sir," she answered quickly before licking her lips and backing her ass into me.

"I think you deserve something with more…" My voice drifted off as I palmed her ass, feeling the plumpness in my palm. "Bite." She shivered against me as soon as I spoke the word.

One thing I knew about my wife, and a line I would never cross, was that she wasn't into pain. Not like some of the women I'd been with. Izzy liked the sting of my palm against her skin. Sometimes, even a slap against her clit sent her into the stratosphere, but never once did she give any inclination that she enjoyed pain.

"You want my hand, Izzy, but I'm not going to reward you." I stepped away, grabbing the black leather crop off the wall. It had the perfect amount of snap that would make her happy and keep my hand from hurting for hours.

"What are you getting?" She turned,

trying to see what I had, but it was hidden behind my back.

"Do you trust me, doll?" I whispered in her ear.

She swallowed hard but nodded her answer.

I walked around to her front and placed my hand against her jaw, dragging my thumb across her bottom lip. "I'd never hurt you."

"I know," she breathed and stared me straight in the eye.

I slid my hand down her neck, over the swell of her breast, and straight down her middle. When I pushed my fingers between her legs, she sagged in the chains and moaned. Izzy was wet. She wanted everything. She loved the anticipation and unpredictability as much as I did.

She spread her legs wider, wanting more contact than I wanted to give, and I stepped backward, taking my hand with me. "First, I want you on your knees. Suck my cock, and maybe I'll spank that pretty round ass while I fuck you."

Her eyes lit up, and she yanked at the chains. "You gettin' a stepladder?"

Using the crop, I slapped the inside of her thigh. Not hard enough to hurt, but enough that it made her yelp in surprise. "Your mouth needs to be workin', not talkin', doll." I dropped the crop to the floor, pulling the lever above her head to allow her to kneel before me, still strapped into the restraints.

She worked quickly despite her restraints, undoing my belt and the zipper on my jeans and yanking them down far enough on my hips to free my hardened cock. She palmed my length, licking her lips in preparation before pressing the tip just beyond her teeth.

I swayed backward, the feel of her mouth so consuming that my legs tingled. Izzy could suck the meanest cock. There was something about watching my mouthy spitfire on her knees, servicing me, that brought me so much happiness, something only another man could understand. Even after over ten years together, I craved her mouth just as much as I lusted after tasting her pussy.

I rocked back on my heels as her fingers bit into the skin of my hips, holding me to her as she pressed forward and pulled back, working my cock like a master herself. At that moment, I was at my weakest. I was a slave to her and her warm, sweet mouth wrapped around my cock.

I tangled my fingers in her long brown hair, holding myself steady as much as keeping her mouth closer to my body. My body convulsed as she swirled her tongue around the head, pulling it deeper into her throat, almost touching the back.

"Mmm," I groaned, wishing she could do this all night, but knowing that it would be impossible for me to last. She knew every spot to hit to send me over the edge faster, and I was powerless to stop her. "Fuck, baby."

Her tiny hand moved between my legs before she cupped my aching balls, pushing me closer to orgasm. My body surged forward, wanting every part of her to be touching every part of me. My eyes drifted over her body, taking in her beauty and nakedness with her legs spread and her breasts bouncing with each thrust forward, impaling her lips around my cock.

Suddenly, I didn't want to play. I didn't want to be the Master with my submissive. I wanted to slide between her legs, lick every ounce of wetness from her body before I pummeled her pussy raw. I pulled back on her hair, removing her mouth from my cock and instantly missing the contact. "Up," I said, motioning with my fingers for her to stand.

She crawled to her feet, standing with her cuffed and chained hands at her side. I quickly removed my clothes before I un-hooked her, taking the restraints off her hands and ankles and lifting her into my arms. "This won't do."

She slid her palm against my chest and

stared up at me. "Maybe you need a spanking." She giggled.

I climbed onto the king-sized bed, holding her in my arms, and laid her gently on her back. "I need to taste you."

Her arms drifted above her head as she stretched out, spreading her legs open with a salacious smile. "Feast," she told me, but I didn't need her permission, nor was I asking for it.

I brought my mouth down, covering her middle with my lips and flicking her clit with my tongue. She quaked underneath me, moaning her appreciation for the pleasure I'd felt only moment ago. We kept our eyes locked on each other as I indulged in her flesh, and she fisted the comforter in her hands.

When my cock couldn't take much more, I crawled between her legs, pressing the tip to her opening and staring down at her. "I love you, doll."

"Jimmy," she said, wrapping her arms

around my shoulder. "Fuck me."

I didn't move because I wanted more than that. She wanted to come, but fuck, so did I.

"I love you too," she finally replied, realizing what I was waiting for and was rewarded for her words with my dick.

I pushed inside. Slow at first, relishing the feel of every inch of her encasing my dick like a vise. My lips crashed down on her breast as she cried out, and her legs wrapped around my waist.

Moments like that, where I was making love to my wife, were still better than any thrill I'd ever had with a submissive at Taboo. They meant nothing to me. They were just a fuck. But Izzy…she was my everything. From the moment I set eyes on her, I knew she'd be mine.

I took her slowly, reminding her who she belonged to as I fucked her. This wasn't just about getting off…this was about us. The connection we'd always had, the spark that had always simmered under the surface, and the unpredictability that kept everything interesting.

The feel of her against me, the way she purred in my ear as I pumped into her sent me barreling toward the edge, and I took her with me. We gasped together. We moaned. We were completely in sync as if we were meant to be together, like this, for eternity.

I STARED UP AT VICTORIA'S SMALL APARTMENT just outside the city limits of Miami. The neighborhood was riddled with old apartments, run-down businesses, and more than a few unsavory types walking the streets.

"Stay in the car and keep the doors locked," I told Izzy, glancing up at the gray stucco building and hoping it was just going to be a quick visit.

After a weekend with my parents, I was more than ready to get home to our boys and back to work. I'd gathered all I could at

Taboo, and we needed to move forward with the investigation, tracking down every lead I'd been able to obtain. The rest would be grunt work, mainly done through computers by tracking the alias Matías had used.

"I'm not staying here." Izzy hopped out of the car before I even had a chance to touch the door handle.

"Damn it," I muttered, jumping out of the Challenger and locking the door as I followed her. "Do you even know where you're going?"

"Nope." She stopped moving, but she kept her back to me as I caught up to her. "All I know is that I'm coming with you."

"Fine, but just stay behind me."

"I will, but I'll keep an eye out."

"For what?"

"Bad guys." She shrugged.

I shook my head and laughed. "You do that." I figured if she kept a lookout, then she wasn't getting into other trouble, so let her have at it.

She followed me up the rusted-out staircase in front of the building, her high-priced heels clicking against the metal with every step. It was a good thing we weren't trying to sneak up on anyone because they would've heard us coming from a mile away.

"Try the handle," Izzy said after I knocked twice with no answer.

I jiggled the handle, but it was locked. I grabbed my phone and dialed Thomas, who answered on the third ring. "Hey, bro. We're about to head back, but I need you to start lookin' into a possible missing person tied to Matías." I rattled off the details, keeping an eye on Izzy as she popped her gum and watched a drug deal happening on the sidewalk by the street.

"How can a single woman live in this shithole?" she asked as soon as I hung up with Thomas.

"I've been in worse places."

"Well, fuck, me too, but I'd never live in a place like this."

"You could always sell your shoe collection if we're down on our luck. We could probably buy a mansion with the money."

I was partially to blame for her monster shoe collection. I'd added more pairs to her closet than I cared to admit. But our agreement was I got to see them on her first, and she wasn't allowed to wear anything else at the time.

She slapped my shoulder as we started down the staircase. "I would never part with my shoes. They're too important."

"So is survival," I reminded her.

"Shoes are my lifeblood."

I rolled my eyes as I opened the car door for her and pushed her up against the frame. "I love them wrapped around my waist when I'm fuckin' ya, but they aren't that important, doll."

"That's like saying blow jobs aren't important." She leaned forward, bringing her lips near mine. "Could you do without?"

"There's nothing sweeter than your mouth."

"That's how I feel about my shoes." She smirked.

"You're supposed to feel that way about my cock, Izzy."

She slipped under my arms, sliding into the seat of the car. "I'll always feel that way about your cock, but you've never said…" She pursed her lips and tilted her head. "'Izzy, you've had too much cock. You may want to stop enjoying it so much.'"

She had me there. I didn't have a good comeback when she put it that way. "Point taken," I said, closing her inside before rounding the hood.

We had a five-hour drive back home, and if I was lucky, she'd lean across the console and take my cock in her mouth while wearing her sexy, overpriced shoes. Soon we'd be back to reality with our boys and their ultimate cockblocking skills.

10

IZZY

Inked ran like a well-oiled machine after fifteen years in business. What started out as fun became one of the most popular places to get a tattoo in the Tampa Bay area. No longer did we sit around waiting for people to walk through the door. Now we were booked over a month out and had a waiting list of clients wanting to be tattooed.

Mike still handled the books and was the same anal-retentive asshole he'd always been about it. His newest thing was a team meeting every Thursday before the clients poured through the doors.

"So, in closing…" Mike paced around the room as everyone played on their phones and ignored him like always. "We should think about bringing on two new artists and another piercer to handle walk-ins."

There was a collective groan, but he finally had our attention.

"I vote nay," Anthony said with his feet kicked up and his face buried in whatever nonsense he was playing on his cell.

Mike stared up at the ceiling and took a deep breath. "Why?"

He had to expect us not to agree with bringing in a stranger. He'd brought up adding more people to the shop before, and we'd always said no. We liked our dynamic and didn't want some young, overeager twentysomething coming in and trying to change everything.

"Just nope," Anthony said, probably to set Mike off.

"I'm good with whatever." I stayed impartial because, at this point, I could use a few more days off here and there, and help sounded kind of nice.

"What?" Anthony finally looked up, giving me an icy glare.

Sometimes, I wanted to take his phone and jam it up his ass. He was so busy chatting with Max or playing games that half the time he was mute when he was around.

"We could use some help around the shop. Maybe we could actually take more time off since we're getting older, and we wouldn't have to be short-handed on those days." I climbed out of the chair and started to prep my station for the first client of the morning. "Plus, more artists means more clients, which means more money."

"We don't need the money," Anthony replied.

"We don't, and we don't need to work either. Wouldn't it be nice to take a day off and not feel like we're shafting the others?"

Joe answered for me, knowing exactly how I felt.

"I don't want to be working every day when I'm sixty, man. Inked eventually needs to have fresh blood, or we'll end up closing the doors someday."

I hadn't thought about that. I assumed someday our children would take it over, but maybe that wouldn't happen. We needed a backup plan just in case they wanted to branch out on their own and not follow in the footsteps of their parents.

"I see I'm outvoted. Just don't bring in some asshole," Anthony said.

"I think we need to hire another female." I smiled.

"I think you're right," Joe said.

The cock/pussy ratio was way off at Inked. Most tattoo shops had a disproportionate number of female employees, and we weren't any different. I could use a little more estrogen around this place to help keep the guys in check.

Mike tossed his notepad on his work station and collapsed in the chair. "It's settled. I'll put out the word and see what happens, but I do have some portfolios already in the office."

"We all have to be in agreement on this person," Anthony chimed in, still being a stick in the mud.

"Shut up, man." Joe turned his back to Anthony and started his prep for the first client of the day.

Anthony shrugged it off, going back to his phone because he'd prepped when Mike started the meeting because he hated Mike's weekly chats as much as the rest of us.

"I'll take a look at them today, Mikey. Just put them out, and we'll all start. Right, Anthony?" I quirked an eyebrow, waiting for him to get mouthy with me, but he didn't.

"Yeah, whatever," he grumbled into the screen of his phone.

Within minutes of Mike flipping the open

sign on the door, our morning appointment arrived, and it was time to dig in and get to work. My first client was the easiest of the day. A small little wrist tattoo that said "I am enough" with a thin cross at the right side. It was beautifully delicate and turned out perfect. The client left satisfied and over the moon excited about her first tattoo. It went so smoothly that I had an hour before my next appointment. I wandered into the office after cleaning my station and started to power through a stack of portfolios that Mike must've been compiling for years.

I opened Facebook and Instagram, figuring it was the best way to see their newest work and a great way to get a feel for the person before they stepped foot inside Inked. I sorted the pile into two stacks—cock and tits.

I opened the first portfolio which belonged to Telula Mabel Bell. The name was a bit wonky, but hey, who was I to slight a person for their name and fucked-up parents. Her line work was decent, but her saturation left a little something to be desired. I clicked through her Facebook profile, and she looked more like a church mouse than a tattoo artist.

We needed to find someone who could put up with the bullshit of not only the clients, but my brothers. The task wouldn't be easy because they were…them.

I tossed Telula to the side and grabbed the next portfolio. Kat West. I liked the name. It was totally made-up, but it was one that sounded like a tatted-up, ballbustin' girl. I flipped through the pages, studying her line work, saturation, and style. Everything looked spot-on and creative. She included some drawings that she'd created specifically for us to show us her range and creativity.

The one thing I didn't want was someone who could only follow a pattern that'd already been created. This shit wasn't paint by number. We needed another *artist* who was going to bring her unique skill and style to Inked along with an established clientele.

Kat's Facebook and Instagram told me everything I needed to know about her. Not only was it filled with her work, but also her family. She had two older brothers and a sister, which put one extra point in her column. If her brothers were anything like mine, I was sure she could handle the Gallo boys without an issue.

Kat had the look too. Long black hair, overdone eye makeup that made her large brown eyes stand out, and the complete rocker chick look that would have the men falling over themselves to get a tattoo from her. As far as I could tell, she was perfect for Inked.

"Izzy. Martin's here," Anthony yelled just as I was about to pick up another portfolio.

Martin was going to be my longest and final appointment of the day. We'd been working on a massive back piece for what seemed like months now. We were in the homestretch, filling it with colors out the ying-yang. I was stoked to see the final product, but we still had another session after this one before we could call it done.

I walked back into the shop to find Martin already lying down with his shirt off and ready. "Hey, Martin. Miss me?"

Martin looked over his shoulder as I sat down, giving me the brightest smile. "I always miss your kind of torture, Iz."

I giggled and patted his back softly. "You love it. You're a pain slut even if you'll never admit it. How many hours do you want to go?"

He tucked his hands under his chin and readied himself. "Do it until I say stop."

Martin Santorini lived about an hour away from Inked, but he said I was worth the drive. He was married with two kids and lived the American dream. He was a Pasco County Sherriff's deputy and looked every bit the part with his flattop haircut and the badass ink that covered his arms. I knew if he pulled me over, I wouldn't argue because he looked too mean to fuck with, even for me.

"I have all day."

"Do your damage, babe."

I loved clients like Martin. He never bitched or whined about the pain and never complained about a damn thing. He lay there with his eyes closed and sometimes chimed in on our conversation with some witty, smartass comment. He'd been a client for years, and he wore at least a half dozen pieces that I'd created specifically for him.

An hour later, Anthony came strolling out the office. "Who is this chick?"

I glanced up and noticed he was holding Kat's portfolio. "I pulled her file. I think she'd be a great fit."

"Her work is amazing."

"I know," I told him, dipping my needle into the blood red as I filled in the drops of blood that were running down the dragon's mouth on Martin's back. "She has older brothers too, so she'll be able to put up with your bullshit."

"Lemme see that." Joe grabbed the portfolio from Anthony's hands and flipped through the pages. "I say bring her in for an interview."

"I'll call her when I'm done," Mike said, pointing to his workstation because somehow, he'd been elected keeper of the business. "I don't want any of you shitheads scaring her off."

Joey tossed it onto Mike's workstation and stalked back toward his area. "If she scares that easily, she's not right."

No truer words. Whoever filled a seat at Inked needed to be ready to give as good as they got. Working with Anthony, Joe, and Mike sure as fuck wasn't easy and I was their sister. I wondered how a newcomer would be able to handle their bullshit. It would be nice to see them choke on their male chauvinist attitudes every now and then.

By the time Martin walked out the door, bloodied and sore, my back ached and I was in need of some serious alcohol therapy and a little girl time. I had texted Suzy, Mia, Max, and Angel when I took a break from Martin's backbreaking tattoo to plan a little something for tonight, and it was the only thing that got me through the day without popping my lid at my brothers.

"Peace out, bitches," I said over my shoulder as I pushed open the door and walked outside.

They weren't too happy to hear about the kid-watching duties each of them would be doing tonight since the mommies were going out without them. Since the kids were older, it was easier for the men to handle them and get them to bed without too much of a fight.

By the time I walked into Caliente, the newest and swankiest Mexican place in Spring Hill, the girls already had a table and had downed almost an entire pitcher of margaritas.

"Well, don't you look like shit today," Max said before I even had a chance to put my ass on the chair.

"Fuck off, Max. You try leaning over for seven hours and look as wonderful as you do after playing with clothes all day."

Suzy started to choke, covering her mouth, and looked at me with wide eyes. I said it. I had no problem going there with my sister-in-law. Yes, she always looked flawless, but hell…if I played dress-up Barbie all day, I would too.

"That shit is hard work, Iz. You try making a meaty man look more like a million bucks than an overstuffed sausage."

I didn't know why, but an image of a guy wearing a sausage costume flashed through my mind, and I started to laugh uncontrollably. Max pushed an already filled glass of margarita in front of me and smiled. "We're celebrating."

"What?" I asked, still laughing and trying to get the drink to my lips without spilling a drop.

"Mia's been nominated for a prestigious award from the state. Something about helping the needy." Max rolled her eyes.

"We're so proud of you, Mia." Suzy grabbed the pitcher and refilled her glass. Thank God she'd grown into a drinker instead of just the fruity umbrella drinks she used to enjoy. I'd always felt like I was going out with a kid instead of a sister.

I set the glass against my lips, taking a small sip instead of chugging it. Tequila and I had never been friends, but there was something about a margarita that made it more copacetic to my system. "Congrats."

"Thanks, ladies. I'm excited our little clinic is finally being recognized. Plus," she said and took a sip of the salty yet sweet drink and winced. "The large grant we'll receive as part of the award will help tremendously."

The entire family was proud of Mia.

She'd accomplished something important and made a real difference in our community. Her clinic gave families an alternative to going to the emergency room and having to mortgage their houses if they were sick. Every single person in our family had volunteered there, especially in the beginning.

"Another round," Angel told the waitress as she passed by our table. "We're not leaving here until we're shit-faced."

"I have Uber on standby," Suzy added with a devilish grin.

I turned to face her with my chin practically on the floor. "You getting drunk, Suz?"

"Tipsy." She laughed. "I don't do drunk well."

I didn't want to be the one to tell her that she didn't do tipsy well either, so I kept that to myself. Suzy's been part of my life for almost fifteen years, and she slowly came over to the dark side, but it wasn't easy. She couldn't pretend to be a good girl after marrying my brother. We knew she was as dirty as the rest of us, hidden behind her sweet smile and wholesome beauty. Over the years, the girls—the ones who sat beside me now—had worn away at her shiny exterior and finally pulled her out of her shell, and her badassery had skyrocketed.

My brothers did well when they picked their wives. Not one of them was a cunty asshole I couldn't stand being around. Each one of them was my friend, probably my best friends, and I was lucky to call them sisters.

"So…" Angel leaned back in her chair. "Izzy, want to tell us about your weekend?"

I placed my drink on the table and smirked. "What did you hear?"

"Not too much. James doesn't like to discuss your sex life, but I know you went to Taboo."

Max sat up straighter and rested her head on her hand. "What's Taboo?"

"Kink club in Miami," Angel answered instead of letting me field the question.

I leaned back, fingering the base of my

margarita glass. "It's the club James used to be a member of a long time ago. We were following a lead in one of his cases. No big deal." I shrugged it off, but I could tell they wanted more, and I hadn't said anything to deter their interest.

"Ooh. Do tell," Suzy said, turning toward me. "Did you meet some of James's old friends?"

"I met some interesting people." I didn't want to talk about it. The ladies always had a million questions, and for some odd reason, I figured they were always picturing me naked with James pulling on a leash. "We're going to hire a new girl at Inked," I said to change the subject.

The table grew silent, and every set of eyes landed on me.

"Excuse me?" Max said, jolting backward.

"I'm sick of being the old chick. We need new employees, and we're starting with a woman."

I crossed my arms over my chest and

stared at them as they gawked at me. By the looks on their faces, I could tell they weren't happy.

"How can we trust someone else around our husbands all day?" Max asked with a little bit of a snarl.

"Yeah," Suzy joined in, usually the quietest of the bunch.

I held up my hands before the lynch mob started. "Have you all gone mental?"

Never had I know any of them to be the jealous type, but I could see the flashes of insecurity behind their eyes as they thought about a woman starting at Inked that wasn't a member of the family.

I needed to quash this before they had a chance to whisper in their husband's ears and we ended up with yet another dick at Inked. "Ladies." I leaned forward, clasping my hands and keeping a straight face. "Calm your tits, please. Your men love you, so there's nothing to worry about. Plus, do you think I'm going to hire someone more beautiful than me?" They didn't look convinced as they glanced at each other and brought their eyes back to mine. "I'll make sure she's married, okay?"

"Married women cheat all the time," Max added with a smug look.

"Oh, please." I slapped my hands on the table. "I'll never make everyone happy, but know this, my brothers love you for some odd reasons, and I'll rip their dicks off if they even flirt with the woman."

Angel grabbed her drink and lifted it to her lips. "She's right," she said before taking a sip.

"Yeah," Suzy said on a sigh. "We trust you, Izzy."

"I got you girls, but I can't deal with another man at Inked. Those three meatheads are enough, and I need a little girl power to even shit up." The table was entirely too quiet still, and I knew I hadn't fully convinced them, so I changed back to the topic I knew they wanted to talk about. "I met the Master that trained James."

They were filled with questions, and all thoughts and insecurities over hiring another female at Inked were forgotten, and we drank until Suzy fell off her chair and it was time to Uber our asses back home.

JAMES

"FINALLY TRACKED VICTORIA DOWN," FLASH said as he breezed into my office just after three in the afternoon.

I peered up from my computer as he slid into the seat across from me. "And?"

"She's safe. She went to visit her mother in Detroit."

"You talked to her?" He nodded and started to shake his foot that hung over his other leg as he sat with his ankle propped on his thigh. "What did she say?"

"Matías did spook her. She decided to

leave town after they spent an evening together. She knew something was off, so she thought it was best to get as far away from him as possible."

"I'll make sure to let the guys at Taboo know she's safe. I know they've been worried."

Flash didn't move even though I'd basically dismissed him. He stared at me, which was awkward.

He'd grown on me over the years. His past with Izzy made it a little harder for me to become friends with him. The whole, he fucked my wife bit kind of grated on my nerves. I won in the end, slipping the ring on her finger and making her mine, but it didn't make it easy to sit across from a man every day who knew exactly how she tasted.

"Something else?"

"I'm going to need to take an extended leave."

"Why? What's up?"

He hadn't taken time off since he started

at ALFA. Sure, he'd taken a few days here or there, but extended time meant a long-term absence and one that would leave a hole in our company.

"Fiona's expecting."

I jumped up from my chair and rounded the desk to shake his hand. "Congrats, buddy."

"Thanks, but she's been put on bed rest. So, until her mother can come down and take care of her, I'm going to be taking a leave."

"What's wrong?"

"The doctor said some mumbo jumbo about an incompetent cervix. Whatever the fuck that means."

"We're all here to help with anything you two need."

"Thanks, James." He gave me a small smile, but I couldn't imagine what he was going through. "I'm excited about finally being a dad and don't want anything to happen to Fiona or our baby."

The last thing I wanted was for Flash to

worry about his place here at ALFA while focusing on the birth of his child. We needed him. I needed him. We didn't run without him, and he'd become an invaluable member of the team.

"I'll talk to Thomas, and maybe you can work from home. We still need your skills and contacts. Would that work for you?"

His face brightened. "That would be great. It would make everything easier. I can't sit there all day and do nothing."

"I get it. I do," I told him because I wasn't a sitter either.

Even when it was my day off, I was always doing something. I didn't like to sit idle with my hand tucked in my pants, watching television. I was a doer. Always had been a workaholic, and it was something I didn't see changing anytime soon.

"Thanks, man," Flash said as he climbed to his feet, looking a lot happier than he had when he walked in.

"Anytime." I waved him off. Although I

was doing it for him, it was in the best interest of ALFA to keep him active and working, especially with a case like Matías's still open.

But then again, there was always an important case we were working on. As soon as a top priority was closed, another one popped up. Our little company Thomas and I started when we finally hit burn-out level after working at the DEA had grown into one of the most well-respected and in-demand investigative companies in Tampa Bay. I never would've believed it possible with the ragtag group of guys we had working with us.

Leaving the DEA was one of the hardest decisions of my life. After years of training and climbing the ladder, getting more and more important assignments, I'd be lying if I didn't admit that I had been a little hesitant walking away. But having Thomas with me and with the clear goal in mind of opening ALFA Private Investigations, I figured, what the fuck, how could it go wrong?

Every agent had a burn-out point, and I

hit it just as Thomas did. Working on the case with the Sun Devils MC was a nightmare. Not only was Thomas's life at risk every single day, but then Izzy's life was in danger too after Flash, being the sometimes dumbass that he was, brought her to Daytona for Bike Week. Naturally, she'd caught the eye of the SD vice president. Thank God Thomas was there to work shit out and keep her safe.

After what was almost a clusterfuck of epic proportions, I was ready to tap out when we did. I'd never regretted the decision either. Being my own boss, surrounding myself with the best and most trustworthy people in the business, and living life on my terms gave me a freedom I never knew when I was with the DEA.

"Am I interrupting?" Ret asked, standing in the doorway as Flash stood near my desk.

I waved him in as his eyes moved from Flash to me. "We're done."

"Thanks again, James," Flash said as he

walked toward the door. "Hey, Ret. Nice to see you back."

Ret gave him a chin lift as Flash passed. "Wanted to talk to you about Matías."

"Whatcha got?"

Ret sat in the same chair Flash had just occupied, looking way more relaxed and comfortable in front of me. "I want to help with catching the fucker."

Ret was our newest addition, although he'd been here longer than a hot minute. He was also Bear's kid, which added some moments that were funnier than shit. But Ret, just like his father, was a man of honor. In his previous life, he was a bounty hunter. He chased down the bad guys using any means necessary and often put his life in danger while doing it. ALFA gave him more security and less chance of his ass getting popped while on the job, although the pay was significantly less, but he didn't seem to mind.

"Well, you know I'm like you and have

spent more than a few nights inside a BDSM club."

I nodded. Ret and I had talked more times than I could count about handling our women. "I do."

"Since he seems to be making the rounds at clubs, I thought I could reach out to my contacts around the country and see if they can help."

He had my attention. I hadn't even thought of asking him to help on the case. I should've known that he had ears and eyes everywhere that could help track Matías as he hopped around the country. "What kind of contacts?"

"I have memberships in or at least have visited every major BDSM club in the fifty states." He rubbed his hands on his jeans with a tiny smirk. "I didn't like to sit in my hotel room at night and watch television, so I filled my downtime with some of the best submissives in the country."

"Busy man."

"Happier than a pig in shit." He laughed, relaxing back into the chair. "I figure I can call my contacts within the clubs and put out an APB to find out where Matías is right now. It may help save us a lot of time and legwork."

Resting my fingertips against my lips, I thought about what he proposed. Matías seemed to be using BDSM clubs as a means to nab women who were already well-versed in the lifestyle. "Do you trust these people?"

"I trust them implicitly, and if there's a bounty involved, they'll be more inclined to find the man."

I rubbed the scruff on my face, staring at Ret and pondering his idea. Money motivated everyone. Even my kids, when I thought it was time for them to get lost so Mommy and Daddy could have a little private time. Ret's idea of offering money out of the ALFA coffers to get people in the BDSM community talking and sharing was a brilliant idea. "How much money are we talking?"

"Five thousand should be plenty to get people salivating and tracking his ass down."

"You got it. Just make sure it's on the DL. We don't want Matías to get spooked and head underground."

"The real question is…do you trust me, James?" Ret leveled me with his stare, the same one that probably had submissives' legs quivering all over the world.

"I do. Make magic happen."

Before Ret could walk out, Thomas strolled in. "I heard there's a party in here."

It fucking seemed like it over the last thirty minutes as people popped in with news and walked out. It had been a nonstop parade, and it always seemed to end up at my desk instead of Thomas's.

"Here's the man of the hour," I said with a little more snarkiness than usual.

"I'm going back to my office. I'll get right on it, James." Ret passed Thomas on the way out.

"Why do you think everyone comes to me

instead of you?" I asked Thomas before his ass hit the chair.

He shrugged it off and laughed. "You're friendlier than I am."

I groaned. "You know I'm a bigger asshole than you."

"I do." He pitched his thumb toward the doorway. "But they don't."

I sighed. "Ret came up with a great idea to sniff Matías out of the shadows."

"The bounty is perfect."

I jerked my head back. "You know?"

"Uh, yeah, fucker."

I twisted my lips because Thomas had gotten one over on me. "You keep sending everyone in here, don't you?"

He laughed so hard he had tears in his eyes. "I always tell them to check with you first."

"You're a complete dick."

He pounded on his chest and smiled. "But you love me."

I grumbled under my breath, but I did

love the man. He was the closest thing I had to a brother. From the day we started training until today, we'd been thick as thieves. I'd say I was closer to him than any of his blood brothers. Spending time away from everyone and keeping secrets left a hole that never would be completely filled. He and I shared experiences that no one else would ever understand, and because of that, we had a different relationship than many normal friends.

The one thing I was most thankful about was that my relationship with Izzy never changed the friendship Thomas and I had. It could've turned into something we would've never recovered from, but he knew the kind of man I was and thought his sister and I were a perfect match. He turned a blind eye when it came to our sex life, thank God, and all he cared about was that I made her happy.

IZZY

"Ma, go sit down. We'll do this," I said as she fussed with everything for the umpteenth time since I'd walked in the kitchen.

"I'm more than capable," she told me, putting me right in my place with her tone that said "don't fuck with me."

"Wouldn't you rather be kissing on your grandbabies?" Mia asked, trying to help.

"I'll kiss them after we have dinner."

My ma had been cooking Sunday dinner

for longer than I could actually remember. I didn't remember a time where she didn't cook for the entire family. Even after she broke a bone or two—we won't get into how that happened because I'm still traumatized—she still slaved away over the stove to put on a spread that would rival any Italian restaurant in the country.

Suzy sat at the island, tearing the already-washed lettuce into smaller pieces and tossing them into a bowl that was bigger than her head. Mia stirred the sauce, making sure it didn't burn because there was nothing that made the men in our family grumpier than a few black flakes in their gravy. Max cut the few loaves of Italian bread into thick, meaty slices. And I took the lasagnas out of the oven so they could cool enough to be cut without falling apart.

As the family grew, the meals had gotten larger. Instead of cooking for a dozen people, now there were so many kids and additions that my parents' kitchen was almost at capacity. If we had a few more kids, Ma would have to buy another oven to prep everything and get it on the table at the same time.

"Mar, come sit with me. Let's talk about tomorrow," Aunt Fran said before sipping her glass of red wine next to Suzy.

Fran was the watchdog of the group. She was the worst cook… Yes, even worse than Suzy, and that was saying something. I always thought they should test her DNA or revoke her Italian card because there was no way that shit couldn't just rub off on her. But somehow, it didn't. The only person in the family who could stomach her food was Bear, and that was because he wanted to keep her happy.

Ma smiled at my aunt and finally decided to sit because we had this down to a science. How could we not after over fifteen years of cooking this obscene feast?

"What time are you picking me up?" Ma

grabbed the bottle of wine and poured herself a hefty glass.

"Let's say eleven."

Suzy grunted as she tore the heart of the lettuce head apart and threw it in the bowl like it had somehow offended her. "Where are you ladies going?"

"I have some tests at the hospital."

Dead fucking silence. All stirring stopped. All chatter evaporated. All movement ended. Every set of eyes in the room focused solely on my mother.

"For what?" I clutched my chest and tried to steady my breathing.

My mother had always been as healthy as a horse. But every year, I'd seen the time wearing on her as she got a few more wrinkles and a couple more gray hairs. I knew that time was ticking and that every day with my parents was a gift, but I was not ready for anything to happen to them. I didn't know if I'd ever be.

"Just some routine tests. Mammogram and all that jazz."

I slid my eyes to Mia because, as the doctor in the family, she could call bullshit faster than me, but I needed to get more information. "And you need a ride for that?"

"Well, no." She lifted the wineglass to her lips and took a giant sip, letting the alcohol sit on her tongue so she didn't have to speak.

"For fuck's sake, Mar. Just tell them. They're not kids."

That was the point where my heart dropped. My mother was being shady, not wanting to answer the questions, and Aunt Fran's comment that we weren't kids told me it was bad.

"Fine," Ma snarled at Fran, showing her anger that her secret was out. "The doctor wants me to have a biopsy on a spot they saw on my mammogram. It's really no big deal, and chances are it's nothing."

I stumbled backward. The weight of her words hit me like a sledgehammer. "Do they think you have cancer?" It was a dumb question. They wouldn't be sending her for a biopsy for anything else, but it felt so foreign it was the only thing that came to mind.

"It's just routine. We're trying to rule out cancer. You know how these things are. As we age, weird shit grows. It's probably benign."

"Cancer?" I asked again like I was stuck on stupid. I was, though. It was the last thing I thought I'd hear today. It wasn't where I thought they were going when I heard them chatting about tomorrow earlier. I figured the two of them were going to Nordstrom's to do some damage to their credit cards. Never in my wildest and darkest nightmares did I think they were making a date to go to the hospital to check my ma for cancer.

My hands shook and my lungs felt tight, like a giant weight had been placed on my chest. I blinked twice, staring at my mother, and felt tears filling my eyes.

Mia placed her hand on my shoulder,

giving it a small squeeze. "It's okay, Izzy. Most of the time, the biopsy comes back benign."

I glanced at Mia as I wiped my eyes. "Did you hear what you said? Most of the time."

"Was the spot they saw large, Ma?" Mia asked, ignoring my special kind of crazy.

"No, it was smaller than a dime. Even if it is cancer, it's small enough that they can cut it out, and they have some fancy pill now instead of regular chemotherapy."

Ma talked about the entire biopsy cancer thing like she was chitchatting about a nail appointment, not like the life-altering test that it very well could be.

"That's good. They've come a long way with the treatments. I'm sure it'll be fine." Mia gripped my shoulder tighter and spun me around. "In the other room. Now."

I nodded slowly, stalking toward the dining room with Mia right on my heels.

"You need to calm the fuck down, girl. You're going to give yourself a heart attack." Mia's brown hair swayed as she talked, waving her arms around between us. "Everything is going to be okay."

"Mia," I whispered and looked back toward the kitchen. "Cancer."

She placed both hands on my shoulders and stared me straight in the eyes. "At her age, there are plenty of treatments. Cancer isn't usually as aggressive in the senior population. As we age, everything slows down in the body, including cancer. Your mom is now in her early seventies, Izzy, and she's the perfect candidate for the chemo pill. This is all only *if* she has cancer. It's most likely nothing."

I opened my mouth to say something, but nothing came out.

"Don't freak out until we know exactly what we're dealing with."

There was nothing scarier than that fucking word. I thought I was pretty badass and could knee-kick any fucker that tried to cross me, but I felt completely helpless to do anything when it came to this. There wasn't a damn thing I could do except wait and see what happened.

"Ladies," Ma said, coming into the room behind me with a smile on her face. Always being the cheerful one of the family and the glue that kept us all intact. "I promise to tell you everything. Izzy, you can come with me to the appointment when I meet with the doctor in a week to go over the results."

"A week?" I groaned. I'd have to live with the fear of not knowing if my mother had cancer for a solid week. That was seven days of pure torture.

"Yes." She wrapped her arms around me from behind and nuzzled her face in my neck. "I'm a tough old bird, baby. Don't cash me out already."

There was only one chick I knew that was tougher than me, and it was my ma. I was every bit her daughter. I thanked God every day that she raised me to be a strong, independent woman instead of a meek and mild mouse who let men walk over her.

I pressed my head against hers and reached up, placing my hand on her arm. I wished I could freeze our lives at this point in time. I didn't want to get older. I didn't want my parents to get any older either. I loved life just as it was and didn't want a damn thing to change. "I'd like to be there for you, Ma."

"You can." She kissed my cheek, lingering a little longer than usual and smelling me like she did when I was a kid. I'd always thought it was odd until I had kids of my own and caught myself smelling them a little too often to be normal. "Now, let's not talk anymore about this. I want today to be like every other Sunday. No bringing this up to the boys either."

I loved that she still called them boys even though they were men. Everybody in the room was over forty, but she refused to think of them as anything other than kids. "I promise, Ma."

"Let's finish dinner and get it on the table before all hell breaks loose."

I tried to be normal. God, how I tried as we placed all the food on the table and served the Gallo army. As I glanced around the dining room, noticing the smiling faces, I wondered how different everything would be without this. Without the dinner. Without my parents. Without all of it.

James squeezed my leg under the table. "Doll, what's wrong?" he whispered in my ear, tickling me with his whiskers.

I plastered a smile on my face and stabbed my fork into the seven-layer lasagna that had so much stuff in it I wondered how it stayed upright. "Nothing, babe."

His grip tightened because I couldn't pull off a fake smile to save my life. "You look like you lost your best friend."

"Everything's fine. We'll talk about it later," I said before shoving a slice of the cheesy noodle goodness into my mouth, basically ending the conversation. But James kept his hand firmly planted on my knee.

If something happened to my ma, I would

lose my best friend. Although I was a daddy's girl to the core, my ma had always been my tether to the important things in life. She didn't spoil me with false compliments or give in to my whims. She forced me to be who I was and made no apologies along the way.

"How's the shop?" Pop asked like he did every Sunday.

"Good. Busier than ever. We're actually talking about hiring someone new," Mike said between mouthfuls of lasagna.

I cringed because that news hadn't gone over so well last night, and I was sure no one had bothered to talk about it, thinking I'd put an end to it before the ball started rolling.

"Izzy set up an interview with the girl for next week," Mike said, without realizing every female in the room besides me and my ma had stopped eating and were glaring at him.

"Oh, she did, did she?" Max stabbed at her meatball, snarling at me as she spoke. "What's her name?"

"Kat." Mike snapped his fingers, forgetting her name for the fiftieth time since I'd brought him the portfolio. "East."

"West," Joe corrected him. "I think you took one too many hits to the head. Your memory is shit lately."

He took the words right out of my mouth. Mike had never been a list-writer or even that smart, but he usually remembered everything. His fighting career hadn't lasted that long, thankfully, or else he'd probably be mumbling nonsense somewhere in a facility that dealt with memory issues. The glory of being an MMA champ wasn't worth losing your marbles, and he already didn't have any extra to spare.

"Yeah. Kat West." Mike smiled, chewing his food with his mouth open.

"Smart business move," Pop said. "Always best to prepare for the future of the company."

The girls were chomping at the bit to say something, I could tell when I looked around the table. But they weren't going to say anything contradictory to my father's words. They knew why we had to hire someone; they just weren't happy that the person was going to have a set of tits attached.

I watched over Mike's shoulder as the children ate outside on the lanai, preferring to be out of earshot as they talked and mostly played instead of eating. They were a mighty crew, requiring a table just as big as the dining room one we sat at to eat outside. Between the entire bunch, there were eleven children, but at times, it felt more like thirty. My parents never seemed to care how loud or rambunctious the kids got, unlike when we were little.

The women sat in relative silence for the rest of the dinner as the guys talked sports and business. Our minds were filled with the knowledge that my mother was going for a biopsy tomorrow and a general unease about the new chick, even though she hadn't even been hired yet. She could be the most boring and unattractive human being ever born, but it still didn't sit well with the girls.

After we cleared the table and washed every dish, I relaxed on a chaise around the pool while the kids chased each other in circles, screaming so loud I waited for the police to get a noise complaint.

"What's wrong, doll?" James asked as he slid behind me and pulled me against his warm, hard body. "Something's off."

I curled into him, needing his secure embrace to help calm my frayed nerves. "It's my mom, James."

He peppered soft kisses along my neck and caused goose bumps to break out across my skin. "Is she okay?"

"She's going for a biopsy tomorrow."

His arms tightened, and he held me closer, bringing his lips next to my ear. "She'll be okay, Izzy. Don't panic."

"How can you be so sure?" I whispered in a haze as I watched the kids lost in their own happy world.

"My mom had one last year, and it was nothing. It's better to find out and catch it early, yeah?"

His words shocked me. He'd never told me that his mother was going in to have a biopsy. I couldn't believe he'd kept that to himself. But then again, he was a man, and he handled shit differently from me.

"Why didn't you tell me?" I stroked the top of his hand with my fingertips, moving across every dip and ridge of it.

"I didn't want you to worry, doll. Why don't you go with your mom so you feel more in control?"

"I plan on it. I can't not be there for her."

"Whatever makes you happy. Remember I'm always here to talk about it. I love you."

He held me tightly, staring at our kids as they ran in circles, doing cannonballs in the deep end and practically flooding the lanai. We sat like that for a long while, not speaking to each other, just being in that moment.

"James, get your ass in here. It's bottom of

the ninth," Anthony yelled out the sliding glass doors, stealing our moment.

"Go," I told him, giving his hand a pat. "I'll be fine. I have the girls to talk to."

They were sitting at the table on the other side of the lanai, chatting about all kinds of nonsense that I had tuned out. I could no longer remove myself from their conversation and sulk on my own without James at my side. My mother would drag me over kicking and screaming if I didn't get my ass in gear and my head on straight.

James gave me a long, slow kiss that made my toes curl, and it made everything, including the noisy kids, evaporate before he pulled away. "I have something tonight that'll make you forget everything," he said with a sly grin.

"Other than narcotics? Because that's the point I'm at, Jimmy."

He laughed softly, lifting me off the ground and letting my body slide down his, feeling all his hardness. "I have something better than drugs, baby."

"I look forward to the challenge, big boy."

I didn't want to burst his bubble, but I wasn't even sure his mighty cock would get my mind off my mother. I'd let him try, though. Because I wasn't a quitter, goddamn it.

After James walked inside, I sat down next to my mother and grabbed the bottle of Jack that I'd set out earlier and poured myself a drink.

"Get that sappy shit out of your system, yet?" Ma asked.

"Ma."

"No, Izzy. Listen to me."

I turned to face her, giving her my full attention because I wanted to hear her pearls of wisdom, and she was going to give them to me whether I wanted to hear them or not.

"Don't worry yourself sick. I'm here. I'm not going anywhere. The doctor is confident that even if it is cancerous, it's easily beatable. I plan to be around for many, many years. Stop putting my ass in the grave before I'm ready. Ya hear?"

"Izzy. Listen to your mother," Aunt Fran said, giving me a stern look. "She's fine. We're all fine. Get your mind off things. Climb that beautiful man of yours tonight and forget about everything else."

Suzy spat out her Coca-Cola as Fran told me to climb James. "I can't," Suzy laughed, trying to wipe away the mess she'd made.

"Come on. If I were young again, I'd give him a run for his money."

"Aunt Fran," Mia gasped and shook her head.

Angel cocked her head and raised an eyebrow. "You know, Bear's not an old man Fran. I hear about some of the crazy shit you two…"

"Don't." I held up my hands. "I don't want to hear about old-people sex."

"Um," Max muttered and gave me a

crooked smile. "We're getting pretty fucking old ourselves."

"Speak for yourself." I twisted my lips and groped my breasts. "These are not the breasts of an old lady."

"That's Victoria's Secret padding, and they're not as perky as they once were," Suzy told me, which caught me completely off guard because she was always the nice one.

"Aren't those bras the best?" Angel asked, pinching at the sides of her breasts, which looked spot-on and spectacular. "They've saved me from looking like an old hag for way too many years."

"Oh, please," I scoffed. "Your tits are always amazing."

Pop walked out, cheering about the Cubs like a proud peacock and like he had something to do with their win. "Did I interrupt?" he asked as all conversation ceased as soon as he walked onto the lanai.

"Talking about tits," Aunt Fran told him,

crossing her arms over hers and waiting for his response.

He didn't say a word. Just strutted back into the living room, closing the sliding door behind him and going back to the guys and the safety of sports talk as opposed to our conversation.

The table erupted into laughter because the look on his face was priceless. Although my dad loved to tease, he didn't want to get into a conversation about breasts with the girls in his life, and we all knew it, including Fran, who just wanted him to leave us alone and not have to hear any more about the Cubs being winners.

"That'll teach him." Aunt Fran smiled.

I knew exactly how she felt. There was nothing like making your brother so uncomfortable and forcing him to slink away to put a smile on your face. She was the master, though, since she had more years perfecting it with my father than I did with my brothers.

"So let's talk about this Kat woman,"

Max said, and that was the end of the fun. She pulled out her phone and started typing away, looking more like Anthony at that given moment.

"What's she look like?" Suzy asked, twirling the straw of her Coke against her tongue. "Is she young?"

"What's the problem, ladies?" Ma asked, drawing her eyebrows downward.

"They're worried some young, hot thing is going to try to steal their man." I rolled my eyes at the sheer stupidity.

"That's ridiculous," Ma said, and finally, I felt vindicated.

"But," Mia started to say when my mother shushed her.

"My boys love each one of you with every fiber of their being. There's no woman who'll make any difference or catch their eye when a man is truly in love with a woman. If you're concerned that someone is going to try to take your place, maybe you need to look in the mirror and see if there's something you're not doing that could put the relationship at risk."

Max smacked her lips together like she'd sucked on a lemon. "I'm not giving him anal."

Suzy snorted, and Aunt Fran almost fell off her chair laughing at Max's statement. My stomach rolled because the last thing I wanted to picture was Anthony fucking Max, especially in the ass.

"Max, doll, I didn't mean to give him that. I'm just saying that you ladies have nothing to worry about." Somehow Ma kept a straight face because Lord knows, the rest of us couldn't. "Don't project your insecurities onto your husbands and this new employee." Ma looked directly at Max and, with a tiny smile, said, "If you're worried, try a little harder in the bedroom, without the ass, of course."

"Oh, what's wrong with a little ass play?" Aunt Fran asked and shrugged. "Keep the man happy. You never know, Max, you may like it."

Moments like these… God, I loved my family. We were the wackiest fucking bunch I knew, and if an outsider were here, they'd probably say we should all have our heads examined. What family talked like this to each other? Mine, of course. I wouldn't have it any other way either. There wasn't a person in this house I didn't love, and I couldn't imagine life without them.

"Suzy, do you like it in the ass?" Max asked Suzy, putting her right in her cross hairs.

Suzy's chair scraped against the cement pavers, and she scrambled to her feet. "I hear Joe calling me," she said before she disappeared inside.

"You're rotten, Max." Angel smacked Max's arm and laughed. "It's why I love you most."

"Well, I love Mia the most. She's the best one out of all of us bitches," I said.

I did love Mia. Maybe not the most because I couldn't pick one over the other, but her calm equaled out my crazy. It's why we worked. She'd always had her shit together since the moment I met her, and I loved spending time with her. Just like earlier when she'd pulled me into the dining room, there wasn't a time when Mia wasn't there for me, and I'd love her forever for being my wing-girl on the crazy train.

13

<h1 style="text-align:center">JAMES</h1>

I stared down at my wife as she lay under me with her hair spread across the pillow and her lips bee-stung and swollen. Caging her in with my arms and filling the space between her legs, I thrust into her repeatedly until she moaned my name and dug her fingernails into my shoulders.

This wasn't about controlling her or using any of my voodoo mind-magic, as she'd called it before. This was about her getting lost in us and forgetting everything else going on outside our bedroom.

"You like that, baby?" I asked. "You love my cock?"

"It's all right," she said and giggled softly.

That smartass comment was rewarded with a quick jab of my dick as deep as I could push it. Far enough that it stole her breath and her fingernails almost punctured the surface of my skin.

"I love your cock. I love your cock," she cried out.

I leaned forward, nipping at her neck where it met her shoulder. The very place I knew caused her to shudder. "Good girl."

She needed this as much as I wanted it. I was pounding into her, so close I could almost taste it, when the doorbell rang.

"Don't stop." She hooked her ankles around my ass, holding me closer to her body and not letting me escape.

I kept going, ignoring the door.

The third time they rang the doorbell, Izzy slammed her hands against the mattress and sighed. "Go get it before the asshole wakes the kids."

She unhooked her ankles from around my body before I climbed off the bed and pulled on a pair of sweat pants. The entire walk down the stairs, I adjusted myself and prayed that my hard-on would go down enough that I wouldn't scare the shit out of whoever was on the other side of the door.

"Who is it?" I asked before I made it to the landing.

"Bebé. It's us."

Fuck. It was my parents. What the hell they were doing here at nine o'clock on Sunday night? Hearing my mother's voice was all my body needed to right itself and for every ounce of horniness to evaporate into thin air.

I opened the door to their smiling faces, holding suitcases. "Mama, what are you doing here?"

Her eyes wandered over my bare chest. "Did we wake you?"

"Of course not. It's early." I grabbed their suitcases from their hands and stepped aside so they could enter.

Looked like we had houseguests who were planning on staying more than a night, judging by the size of their bags. We'd had a separate wing added to the house with a small in-law suite for when my parents came to visit. We'd thought it would be more often, but it had so far been only occasionally, especially around holidays when they came to stay a few days before returning to the safety of Miami.

"Come in. Come in."

"I hope we didn't interrupt anything," Papi said as he walked inside and took off his hat before smoothing out his hair.

"No. We were just relaxing," I lied and caught a glimpse of Izzy walking slowly down the stairs.

"Hey," she said in a cheerful tone like I hadn't just been balls deep in her. She was good. She had been all worked up, but it didn't show except for her lips being slightly swollen and redder than usual. "You came." She smiled softly, padding across the hardwood floor to wrap my mother in an embrace.

My mother glanced at me over Izzy's shoulder and winked. "James told us about your mother, and I thought I'd come spend a few days with you until I know you're all right, *hija*."

Izzy hugged her tighter, and I waited for her to turn around and smack me in the stomach. Instead, she whispered, "Thank you," in my mother's ear.

"Son."

"Papi." I motioned toward their suite with the suitcases still in my hands. "Let's get you squared away while the girls talk."

My father followed me down the hallway, stopping every few feet to take in the photos of the kids that Izzy had hung along the walls. "They're getting so big."

"They are. They're going to be so excited to see you both."

"Do they have school tomorrow?"

"No, it's spring break, so they're home all week."

"Your mother will be happy." My father smiled and tossed his hat on the bed before sitting down. "That drive is a pain in the ass."

I placed the suitcases next to the dresser at the foot of their bed and turned to face him. "I know. Thank you for coming all this way for Izzy."

"You know how much we love Isabella."

They did too. When I texted my mother earlier this afternoon after Izzy told me about her mother, I'd never expected them to get in the car and head straight here. They must not have even hesitated since I sent my text a little over six hours ago, and even going at breakneck speed, it took over five and half hours without stopping from door-to-door.

"I know she appreciates it. I appreciate it."

"We'll spend time with the kids this week until you two are sick of us."

I laughed, but usually after five days, I'd had my fill of my space being invaded and needed alone time with my wife. "Stay as long as you want. Do you want a drink?"

"Ahh," he said before licking his lips. "I could go for a nightcap."

"Let's go out on the lanai and talk for a while."

When we made our way back into the main part of the house, Izzy and my mother were already outside with two bottles of wine, the Jack Daniel's, and Dad's favorite brandy.

The sticky spring air blasted me in the face as soon as I opened the sliding door and stepped outside. My mother and Izzy glanced up before going back to their conversation as my father and I took the empty seats on the other side of the table.

Mama placed her hand over Izzy's on the table. "Don't be worried, dear Izzy. I remember when I had mine done. I thought the worst, but everything turned out okay. I'm sure it'll be the same for your ma."

Izzy smiled sweetly at my mother. "I'm so glad you're here."

"I'll always be here for you. You're every bit as much my daughter as he's my son."

They shared a moment, and my father and I sat silently, watching them in silence. Something my father rarely did because the man loved to talk.

"How long are you staying, Mom?" Izzy asked.

"As long as you'll have us. We're going to look at condos while we're here."

"I want you closer, and I know the kids do too."

"What about James?" She turned to face me with one raised eyebrow and a small smile.

"Of course I want you around here. I hate that you're so far away."

"It's settled, then. We'll find someplace

here so we can spend more time with our family."

"Let's drink to it," Papi said, grabbing the bourbon and snifter that Izzy must've set out for him.

"Just one before we retire and you two get back to relaxing." Mama smirked.

Whatever Izzy and I were doing before they'd arrived was over. But the plus side was that her mind was no longer dwelling in dark places. My mother wouldn't allow Izzy any time to worry. My parents being here was the best thing that could've happened to us this week.

"It's quiet without Flash, ya know?" Bear said, sitting down to our Monday morning meeting to go over the week's assignment load.

"Don't be an asshole. He's not loud," Morgan told Bear as he straightened the pile of files he had in front of him. "Not like you, at least. If you weren't here, we'd probably finally enjoy some peace and quiet."

Bear touched his moustache, running his fingers through the hair that was longer than usual as he stared at Morgan. "You'd miss my beautiful face."

Morgan rolled his eyes. "Don't push your luck."

"Who's your daddy?" Bear teased, elbowing him in the arm.

I cracked up. Morgan fucking hated when Bear reminded him about their unique relationship. But the one thing I did know was that Morgan respected Bear and had actually grown to love the man. Who couldn't? He treated Fran like a queen and had turned out to be the best possible match for her.

Kind of like me and Izzy. The strong Gallo women needed someone who was stronger than them to keep them in check, or they'd end up halfway to crazy town. Out of the three ladies—Maria, Izzy, and Fran—I'd say Fran had to be the mouthiest, bossiest woman in the family. And that was saying something, knowing Izzy as well as I did.

Thomas sauntered into the conference room wearing a white dress shirt slightly unbuttoned at the top and a pair of perfectly pressed black dress pants.

"Hot date?" Frisco teased Thomas before he had a chance to sit.

"It's my anniversary, and I'm taking my girl out to dinner after work today."

"An expensive dinner," Angel said from the doorway after she popped her head into the room to say good morning. "I'm only working a half day today, boys, so you're going to be on your own this afternoon."

"We got this," Bear told her with a chin lift and a flirtatious wink.

"Does anyone need anything before I seal you inside?" she asked.

She made it seem so ominous, as if we were being sequestered like the papal conclave at the Vatican when electing a new pope. We were only closing the door so potential clients who arrived early for their appointments didn't overhear us.

"We're good, baby. Thanks," Thomas said before he started to slide folders down the table for each of us to take.

Angel closed the door and headed back to the front of the office to man the phones and keep us organized. It wasn't an easy task either. Keeping seven of us in check had to be a pain in the ass, but she always had a smile on her face and never hassled us for being the assholes that I knew we were.

"Let's start with Matías. Where are we with him?" Thomas asked as we flipped through the extra-thick folders filled with assignments and details outlining the current status of the case and any headway that had been made.

Ret spoke first. "I have feelers out to all my community contacts. I expect to hear something today. We should be able to move soon."

"Let us know as soon as you hear something," I told him.

"I will, boss." He smiled.

"Next order of business. What cases are we closing out this week?"

"I have a hell of one that I can finally say is over. Cheating husband and shit got ugly."

Bear loved those cases. Anything that involved salacious acts, he'd call dibs on before anyone else could claim the cases. I didn't know if it was the possibility he'd get a sneak peek into their bedroom antics or if it was catching someone red-handed that made him happier. Either way, he was up to his neck in cases like that, which left the best stuff for the rest of us.

I loved working here. I loved the people Thomas and I had surrounded ourselves with. There wasn't a better crew around to help solve cases, and some of them didn't mind stepping over the line of legality to make shit happen…especially Bear.

I was damn proud to call ALFA Private

Investigations mine and the guys around this table my dysfunctional and slightly fucked-up family.

Before the meeting ended, Ret's phone started vibrating nonstop and dancing across the table. "I have to take this," he said, excusing himself from the room.

Ten minutes later, when everyone had gone back to their offices, Ret walked back into the conference room with a huge, shit-eating grin. "Found the fucker."

I rubbed my hands together, ready to go get his ass right now. "Where is he?"

"He's been frequenting a club in Jacksonville called Forbidden a few nights a week and has been there the last two weekends."

Thomas tapped his pen against the table-top, leaning back in his chair and swiveling from side-to-side. "I can't believe he's still in Florida."

"He must not have heard about my trip to Taboo. When should we head out?"

"Let's get our ladies and head up there

Friday. We may have to be gone a few days until he shows up. Is that okay, Thomas?"

"Wait." Thomas straightened, and his face grew serious. "You're going to take Izzy again?"

I shrugged. "Yeah. We need the ladies with us to maintain our cover."

He scrubbed his hand down his face, pinning me with his gaze. "I don't like it."

"Have I ever let anything happen to her?"

Fuck, I killed a man for her. Rebel deserved that bullet to the head for messing with my family and trying to hurt Izzy. I'd do it again in a heartbeat if it meant keeping her safe. His death should've weighed heavy on me. Taking a human life was supposed to be a life-altering thing, even if it wasn't the first one I'd taken, but his death meant nothing to me. I felt no remorse or sadness when his light was extinguished.

"I trust you. Just be careful. If there's any sign of trouble, get the fuck out."

"I'll be there with them, Thomas.

Nothing will happen. I know the owner of the club, and we'll be in good hands," Ret stated, holding the back of the chair at the opposite end of the conference table, oozing with confidence.

But if I was being completely honest, a man like Matías should never be underestimated. I knew how quickly shit could go south, and the last thing I'd ever do was put my wife in a situation she couldn't handle.

14

IZZY

TRACE RAN DOWN THE HALLWAY OUTSIDE MY bedroom, giggling as Grandma chased him. I sat blissfully relaxed in my bathtub, not worrying a second about the kids. Mrs. Caldo knew how to get the crew in check, but just like my ma, at times, she just let them run wild.

Her being here the last forty-eight hours had been a godsend. My ma didn't have any complications during her biopsy, and the doctor seemed fairly confident that it wouldn't come back malignant, but we wouldn't know for sure until the lab had studied the sample and given the all clear. Until then, I wouldn't be able to fully relax, knowing there was a small chance that my mother had cancer.

I didn't have any early morning appointments at Inked, and I took the opportunity to pamper myself a little. It was a luxury I didn't often have with three young boys running around the house and getting into Lord knows what while I closed myself away from it all.

I had done it once, and Rocco ended up with a broken arm when he and Mello were playing tag on the staircase. I learned my lesson that day, after spending seven agonizing hours in the emergency room until they put a cast on him. They gave him pain meds to make him feel better, but I was the one who really needed a Xanax after the experience.

I closed my eyes when Trace's scream trailed off, and Mrs. Caldo's footsteps on the staircase grew light. I could get used to this life. She cooked and cleaned, even though I begged her not to, and she made me wish that James would agree to hiring help around the house. He'd give me some song and dance about letting strangers into our home, but I swore the man just liked my cooking a little too much.

That was my failure. I never should've let him know I could cook. I should've been like Suzy. The woman was basically barred from the kitchen unless Joe was feeling particularly daring and let her try her hand at a new recipe—which always ended up being an epic failure. I could've had a chef or we could've eaten out every night, but I had to ruin everything by showing him I had mad skills in the kitchen.

My phone buzzed, but I ignored it. There was nothing that couldn't wait while I relaxed, enjoying the last five minutes I had in the bathtub before I had to drag my ass into Inked to interview Kat.

It buzzed again, and I groaned. I should've turned the vibrate feature off so nothing would interrupt me. I glanced at my phone and saw a text from my sister-in-law, who was still freaking out about the very possibility of Kat coming to work at Inked.

Max: She's too pretty.

I rolled my eyes and slid down the back of the tub, almost putting my entire head underwater. What's wrong with my sisters-in-law? Having another woman at Inked was a good thing. They were acting like every woman in the world wanted to steal their man. News flash…they were not that amazing.

I should know.

I'd spent more years of my life with my brothers than any of them had currently been in a couple. Joe, although I adored him, was broody and bossy as fuck. Mike was a goofball with a huge heart, but he was too much into his body and how veiny he could be for my liking. Then there was Anthony. My favorite and the biggest asshole of them all. I think I loved him most because he was usually too busy with his own shit to get on my ass about little things like the other guys. Thomas… well, he was older and had been basically MIA with the DEA since I was a kid. He and I weren't as close, but he never once told me what to do. He knew I wouldn't listen anyway.

I dried off my hands, taking my time, as another message came rolling in, but this time, it wasn't Max.

Suzy: Good luck today. I'm sure you'll do the right thing.

Ah. That was classic Suzy. She was being passive-aggressive, and I was sure she'd chosen those words very carefully before sending them. Before Mia could send a separate message, I hurried and sent out a group text.

Me: Relax, bitches. I'll make sure she's a lesbian.

I snorted a little because I couldn't and wouldn't ask her sexual orientation, but I was sure it would make my girls feel better thinking I would.

Max: A pussy licker sounds perfect.

Mia: We trust you.

Suzy: I don't care about that.

Suzy lied, and I was sure everyone in on the text knew it.

Me: Max, maybe you need to give Anthony anal and you'll feel better.

A text came in only seconds later.

Max: Fuck you, Iz. It'll make him feel better, but he ain't getting near my ass.

Suzy: You're missing out ;)

Mia: Bahaha. SMDH. Poor guy.

Max: You give up the ass, Mia?

Mia: I don't kiss and tell.

Suzy: I thought we all did.

Me: Suzy's a hoe.

The texts were flying fast and furious now.

Suzy: Takes one to know one.

Me: Peace out. I'll update you later. She could be a complete asshole.

Mia: Anthony could use her, then.

Max: Fuck off, Mia.

Mia: ;)

I closed the window and placed my phone

on the counter before I dried off and tried to get motivated. Maybe taking a bath hadn't been the best idea. I was too relaxed and ready for a nap, not work.

By the time I kissed the boys goodbye and left them with James's parents, I was already running late. I drove a little too fast in my souped-up minivan, if there was such a thing, and made it to Inked five minutes faster than usual.

"I'm here," I announced as I walked through the front door of the shop.

Sitting in the waiting room was Kat West. She could be a pinup for *Inked Magazine* without a doubt. She was drop-dead gorgeous with pastel pink hair, a recent change, based on her Instagram profile. When she rose to her feet and towered over me with her long legs that seemed to go on for miles, I knew the girls would hate her.

"I'm Kat." She smiled and held out her hand to me, and I shook it a little too manlike after being around my brothers for so long.

The girl had a smoking hot body. Big tits, long, thick legs, and totally curvy hot and our clients would go gaga over her.

"Izzy Caldo, one of the owners of Inked."

"I love your work," she said.

"Thank you." I couldn't help but smile. Hearing from another artist that they loved my work was the biggest compliment there was. "Your work is amazing too. I was quite impressed with your portfolio."

"Thank you." She blushed, batting her superlong fake eyelashes and biting down on her bottom lip.

Lord. She had all the right moves to keep the customers coming back for more. There wasn't anything about this woman that didn't scream sex. I'd have to lie my ass off to my sisters-in-law and assure them that she only licked pussy and totally batted for the other team before they chased her away.

"Come on back and meet the guys, and when they're done, we'll start the interview."

Much to my shock, when we walked into the back room, everyone was cleaning their stations and just about ready to start. All eyes in the room turned toward us, and all movement stopped.

I wondered what they thought of Kat and if they felt the sex-kitten ooze off her like I did.

"That's Joe, Mike, and Anthony." I pointed to each one of them, pausing between their names so they could acknowledge her.

"It's a pleasure to meet y'all," she said in her best Southern twang.

"We're happy to have you interview with us, Kat," Joe said as he walked toward her to shake her hand.

"Max is going to kill me," Anthony whispered in my ear as Joe and Kat spoke to each other.

"I have a plan."

"It better be good."

"Well…" I trailed off as I rubbed my

cheek and sighed. "I wouldn't say it's good, but it buys us some time."

"She's way too beautiful for Max to be okay with this."

If James were hiring her to work at ALFA, I'd probably worry for about three seconds until he spanked my ass pink and reminded me that he owned me and me alone. I'd never once worried he'd stray, and the same went for him not worrying about me. I was completely satisfied and happy, but I wondered if my brothers could say the same about their relationships after so much angst about another female being in close proximity on a daily basis.

"Maybe you need to man up and remind your wife how much you want her."

"How? I already spoil her rotten."

"Figure it out, old man, but the woman is seriously having trust issues with us hiring a girl."

"I know," he groaned.

Two hours later, Kat was hired.

When she finally walked out the door, Anthony turned to me. "What's the plan for our ladies? They aren't going to like her at all."

"Well." I glanced up at the ceiling and relaxed back into my chair, turning it from side to side. "We're going to tell them that she's a lesbian."

Mike started to choke and slapped his chest while clearing his throat. "Is she?"

"Fuck if I know, but it sounds good." I shrugged.

"Suzy doesn't care. I don't need to lie to her." Joe seemed so sure of himself, but that meant Suzy hadn't been expressing herself like she did to the rest of us.

"Listen up. I spoke to all your wives, and they're all uneasy about Kat. I don't know what's going on at home, but you boys better step up and start being the men your women need."

"What more can we do?" Mike asked, clueless and cute.

"Anthony." I looked in his direction,

waiting for him to look up from his fucking screen. "Put the goddamn phone down at home and make sure you pay more attention to Max. Joe, wine and dine your woman, you know she loves to be pampered. And Mike…" I stared at him for a minute, wondering what pearls of wisdom I could give him. "Maybe stop kissing your biceps as much and start kissing on her more."

"Izzy." Mike put his hands on his hips and glared at me. "I love Mia more than anything. I quit fighting for her. Don't you think I treat her like a queen at home?"

"I'm sure you all do. But right now, with Kat just starting, you need to be extra lovey-dovey. Shower your woman with so much love that it leaves little doubt about where her husband's heart lies."

"Got it," Joe said with a quick nod. "I won't let her out of bed all weekend."

I held my hand up and closed my eyes. "I don't need details. Just take care of your shit, and remember Kat's a lesbian."

Anthony shook his head and laughed. "This should be interesting."

"Anthony, I think your life depends on it, buddy. Max can be downright scary sometimes."

"I'll handle her."

That statement earned a laugh from everyone in the room. The only person who handled Max was Max. Anthony could try to sell that lie, but we all knew the truth. The woman had mighty big balls, and I totally girl-crushed on her for it.

The next few weeks at Inked were going to be real interesting. I wouldn't let my sisters-in-law derail my plans for getting a little more tit power in the shop. I was sick of being the only female and done with having to deal with my brothers alone. In the end, they'd see the wisdom of my ways.

This weekend, we were heading to Jacksonville to hunt down Matías, and hopefully, all hell won't break loose without me around to handle it. But more than likely, I'll return to a shitshow, knowing my brothers. They'd never been good liars, and I'd never ordinarily ask them to lie to their wives, but I knew it was in everyone's best interest if they followed the program and labeled Kat West our in-house lesbian.

15

JAMES

RET AND I CARRIED THE BAGS IN FROM THE cars as the girls settled into the hotel rooms. The sun had just disappeared behind the Jacksonville skyline, casting shadows in the parking lot and giving us some relief from the heat.

"Women pack way too much shit," Ret said, hoisting Alese's duffle bag higher over his shoulder to free his hands for her other two suitcases.

Izzy wasn't a lightweight when it came to packing either. This time, she helped me pick out her outfits because she said she wasn't sexy enough last time. She'd spent a few hours researching Forbidden and found it to be a trendier club than the old shit-in-the-wall Taboo. She wanted to look every bit the part of a pampered submissive.

"Shit never changes as they age either."

We should've grabbed a cart with the amount of luggage we'd packed, but it gave us a few minutes alone to talk about our plan of attack tomorrow at the club.

"We have to meet Connor at noon to learn the layout of Forbidden. I don't want there to be an inch of the club you're not familiar with when we're there with the ladies. Matías is too dangerous for us not to be prepared."

We strutted through the lobby, looking like every other man in the place, heading to our rooms, shouldering the brunt of the work.

I jabbed at the elevator button with my elbow, not willing to put anything down because it wasn't easy to balance everything to begin with. "Agreed. We'll do a late breakfast and take the women with us. It's important that they're filled in because I'm sure they're already nervous."

Luckily, our rooms were near the elevator, and we didn't have far to travel when we made it to our floor. "Meet downstairs for dinner in ten?" I asked before kicking open the hotel room door that Izzy left ajar even though I told her never to do that.

"We'll be ready," Ret said before his door opened.

Alese stepped into the hallway and plucked the smallest bag from his hands. "Let me help you."

Ret looked at me and shook his head. The last two feet wasn't the time we needed help, but at least she offered. Izzy was nowhere to be found, which meant she was probably talking on the phone, checking on the boys.

I dropped the bags as soon as I made it through the door, and Izzy turned around, giving me her signature glower. I jumped on the bed, trying to lighten the mood and wanting to relax for ten minutes.

Izzy walked out on the balcony, resting against the railing as she chatted on the phone. Based on the way her arm was flailing about, it was a heated conversation too.

"Fuckin' Mike," she said, walking back into the room.

"What happened?"

"He told Mia that Kat wasn't a lesbian."

"Um," I mumbled because clearly, I was missing an entire piece of the conversation. "And that's a problem, why?"

She sat down next to me and started to stroke my leg. "The girls are mad we hired a woman, so I told the guys to lie."

"A little higher." I winked, wishing we had time for a quickie before we headed to dinner.

She slapped my leg and shook her head. "I'm sure I'll be walking funny by the time the weekend is over."

"We'll have to see. If Matías shows his

face tomorrow, the weekend may be over before we ever have a chance to play, doll."

She pouted as her strokes grew longer, and her fingertips grazed my cock. "But I was looking forward to some more us time."

I pulled her down on top of me, bringing her lips close to mine. "Baby, once we're free and clear, you can have all the us time you want. We just have to be on our toes. I can't be balls deep inside you and miss Matías. That would be hard to explain."

"True." She frowned and sat upright, escaping my kiss.

"So what's this about Kat?"

"She's hot. Like superhot and spunky. The girls are livid that we hired her, so the only thing I could figure out is to tell them she's gay."

"You knew that shit wouldn't fly."

She grunted. "Dumbass Mike and his big mouth. I swear I should knock some sense into that boy."

"It won't help."

Izzy climbed on top of me, pressing her cunt against my cock, teasing me because she knew she could and there wasn't a damn thing I could do about it now. "Maybe if you're a good boy." She was turning the tables on me, and I liked it. "I'll suck your cock later."

I grabbed her around the waist and undulated my hips. "Maybe if you're a good girl, I'll let you."

I wanted to strip her naked and spend the night licking every inch of her skin, but the knock on the door ended that fantasy.

"Ready?" She pulled her shirt down far enough to show me her killer rack.

"Baby, I was born ready."

She took her time climbing off me, making sure to make it as torturous as possible as she slid down and stood.

"If you don't behave, you're going to suck my cock until your jaw locks up."

"You talk a big game," she said over her

shoulder as she turned the handle to a waiting Alese and Ret.

My head throbbed as we walked into Forbidden just after noon. Last night, we all had too much to drink and were moving slower than usual.

"Welcome." Connor, the owner of the club, met us at the door to usher us inside. He was a stout man, standing about eight inches shorter than me, with a pot belly and a beard that touched his chest.

"Thanks for doing this." Ret shook his hand, towering over the man.

Ret had filled me in on Forbidden and Connor's background. He used to own a bar in town and was an active participant in the swinger's scene in Jacksonville. When the BDSM explosion happened, he decided to open his own club and mix his two favorite activities—drinking and sex.

Connor had a partner in the business, a former Navy SEAL named Trent Newsome, who was interested in helping us nab Matías. He was waiting inside the main lobby as we entered. "Welcome," Trent said with a curt head nod.

He sized me up, and I did him. The man looked like every other hard-core military special forces person I'd ever met. Strong jaw, big muscles, perfect posture, and lacked any type of emotional facial expression as he stared at Ret and me.

Then his eyes wandered to Izzy and Alese, and he finally cracked a smile. "It's a pleasure to meet you, ladies."

"I'm Alese." She almost curtsied as she bowed her head and stared down at the floor.

"Izzy," my girl said, holding out her hand and looking him straight in the eye.

Attagirl. I didn't like the way he looked at Alese and Izzy, but I knew one thing for sure...Izzy wasn't going to take any of his shit if he tried anything. Her brothers taught her well, and I was lucky I had come out un-scathed when we first met.

He extended his arms, flexing to show off his power. "Welcome to Forbidden."

But men like Trent pissed me off. If you were powerful, good for you. But there was more to power than strength and bulk. To in-fluence someone with words was the biggest high, not by physical force. I liked to think men like Trent never came out on top.

"Thanks for helping us, Trent." Ret pulled Alese close to his side, staking his claim, and I did the same with Izzy because I didn't play games when it came to my wife.

"The last thing we need is a human traf-ficker lurking around our club. I'll do any-thing to help put his ass behind bars."

Connor stepped in front of Trent, maybe as annoyed as I was with his display of bull-shit. "Let's get inside, and I'll give you a tour before you can spend a few hours wandering around on your own."

"Sounds great," Ret told him.

Connor opened the door, and we walked inside the common area with Trent close behind us.

"Matías spends about an hour in this part of the club until he convinces someone to join him in a private room," Connor said as soon as the door closed behind us.

Forbidden was an upscale club with modern touches and one of the nicest I'd been inside of in Florida. The black marble floor and blood-red walls matched the leather furniture that was in the center of the room. On the far right was a viewing platform with a St. Andrew's Cross and shackles hanging from the ceiling just a few feet away.

"We have a lot of members who are into voyeurism. We make sure to have plenty of areas for them to live out that fantasy."

To the left was the bar, lining the entire wall of the club, with built-in stools and a sleek cement top. Behind the bar was a wall-to-wall mirror that could give any drinker the full view of the action going on behind them.

Straight in front of us was an area with cages and stockades.

"Ah, our area for public humiliation." Connor came to stand next to me. "It's become quite popular lately."

It was one thing I could never get into. I wanted to fuck and control, not humiliate the person I was with. But there were plenty of submissives and slaves that were into that kind of thing.

Izzy gripped my arm tightly, pressing her body flush against me. "Um, fuck that."

"Let me show you the private rooms, and then we'll let you be to do whatever you want."

From the outside, the club didn't look large. But it extended into an endless maze of private rooms and smaller public play areas. Each spot had its own theme or purpose, and everything was top-notch. No cheap, shitty BDSM furniture that looked overused. The amount of furniture and apparatus in the club was mind-boggling.

Cages, benches, vacbeds, and bondage chairs were everywhere, along with beds and exam tables in too many rooms to count. This was a playland for anyone in the lifestyle.

So far, the operation at Forbidden was impressive.

"Any questions?" Connor asked after we walked into the last small play area tucked away at the end of the hallway.

We stood around the circular bed that could probably fit ten people easily and must have made for quite a scene.

I pulled Izzy close, not wanting Trent to be anywhere near her. "How do you monitor everything?"

Connor crossed his arms in front of his chest and glanced upward. "All public areas have closed-circuit television monitoring, and the private rooms have cameras on the doorways with a two-way intercom in case there's an emergency. We have designated Masters who walk the hallways and public areas at all times to stop anything from getting out of hand."

Ret stared up at the camera as if he'd never noticed them before. "Can you show us the surveillance room?"

"Sure. We don't keep tapes of anything to protect the security and anonymity of our members, but they're monitored every moment the club is open for business," Connor said, motioning for us to follow him back toward the public area where we'd started our tour.

"You like it here?" I whispered in Izzy's ear as we walked.

"It's amazing," she said, looking up at me with a wicked smile. "I want to use more than a few of these rooms."

"Maybe we'll come back if we don't get any time to experiment."

"Let's hope we catch the bastard tonight, and then we can have one day to play," she told me as we stood outside the nondescript door.

"In here is where we have twenty monitors, along with the intercom system. It's really an amazing thing, and I don't know of a club within three hundred miles that has this kind of setup."

I glanced around the room, taking in the sleek flat-screen televisions lining the one wall. "You've done an amazing job with the club, Connor."

"It's my pride and joy." He smiled brightly. "Now if you'll excuse me, Trent and I have a few things to discuss. We'll let you be, and feel free to holler if you have any questions."

"Thank you," Ret said, looking between the two men before they walked out.

"Should we set up camp in here?"

I rubbed my face. "I think it's best if one of us is on the floor while someone is in here surveying the entire club."

"We'll be in the club," Izzy said quickly, a little too overeager but completely in step with her personality.

"Works for me. Let's walk through it a few more times until we have the layout memorized, and then we can leave for a few hours. They don't open until eight."

"Just enough time to get ready." Izzy laughed.

I peered down at her and gripped her ass roughly in my hand. "Woman, it better not take you seven hours to prepare."

"Baby," she said, running her fingernail down my bicep. "Not all prep is bad."

If prep meant my cock inside of her, I was all about her taking her time. "Whatever you want, doll."

"Let's do this," she said, walking out of the room before the rest of us and leading the way like she always tried to do.

16

IZZY

I PULLED AT MY COLLAR, FEELING LIKE IT WAS more a noose than a decoration. It never bothered me before, but Forbidden was so crowded that I felt claustrophobic. I'd been touched by more people walking by than I had been the last time we visited Disney World.

Based on the number of people here, I'd say it was the most popular place in town and that it had become a destination spot for people in the lifestyle who visited the area.

Connor decided to join James at the bar

for a drink while Ret and Alese manned the security room. I sat behind James, kneeling on the floor in the shadows. The dim lighting near the bar area allowed me to look around without being caught by other Masters scattered throughout the common area.

Matías hadn't shown his face yet, but the night was still young. My knees ached, and I hoped I wouldn't be sitting like this for the next six hours. But at least the scenery was spectacularly sexy.

I just couldn't watch the people who were being put into the stocks and other contraptions to be humiliated. I couldn't wrap my head around why they found it a turn-on. The last thing that made me want to come was when someone was telling me what a slut I was and trying to shame me as I kneeled naked and in front of a group of people.

The stage directly across from me had already had one couple use the St. Andrew's cross, and after a quick cleaning, a new twosome stepped up on the stage. This time, a woman wouldn't be tied to it, but a man. The Domme had on a tight black corset with her breasts spilling out over the top and a pair of skintight black leggings that were partially covered up by her freshly polished over-the-knee boots.

She looked powerful, amazing, and completely in charge of the man. He stared at the floor, stripped bare and waiting for his whipping, and he didn't make a sound as a crowd gathered around the staging area to watch. I almost felt bad for him, but his hard-on told me he was enjoying every minute of it.

I was lost in the scene before me, forgetting that I was supposed to be looking for Matías, when James tugged on the leash, yanking my head sideways. I couldn't help myself as I glared up at him and snarled.

Just as I opened my mouth to say something, he pinned me with his icy stare. "Watch for him. We can't take our eyes off the real reason we're here," he said.

I sighed and went back staring from the

shadows and surveying the room. But my eyes kept drifting back to the man being whipped and then fondled and the group of people whispering to each other with excited smiles as they watched.

Minutes later, James yanked the chain again, but this time I couldn't keep quiet. "What the fuck?" It just came out. I couldn't stop it no matter how hard I tried to remember that I wasn't to speak unless given permission.

A pair of shoes stepped into my line of sight. A very expensive pair of shiny black shoes, probably Versace, based on the details. Slowly, my eyes traveled up the man's well-tailored dress pants to his expansive chest and settled on his face.

Matías.

"Are you being mistreated, li'l one?" he asked in a thick accent with his cold, dark eyes boring into me.

I turned my gaze downward. "No, Sir."

"I've been watching you for some time," Matías said.

James had already swiveled around on the stool and was standing to my side. "Can I help you?" He wrapped the leash around his hand two more times, shortening the space between him and me.

Matías motioned to me with his hand. "It looks like your submissive is unhappy."

Fuck me.

"She's in training. Back off."

"Ahh. I've been known to break a sub or two. Maybe you could use help, no?"

"She's a feisty one," Connor said from behind me.

I almost snorted at that statement. Feisty didn't even begin to describe me, but I'd roll with it.

"Connor, tell the man how good I am at training newbies."

I was sure the fucker was amazing. It was pretty damn hard to steal a woman off the streets and turn her into a sex slave without using means that were deplorable and cruel.

"He's the best I've ever seen, James."

James stepped forward, moving closer to Matías. "You don't get to have sex with her unless I approve. Understood?"

Wait a minute. What the what?

James was trying to get Matías into a room alone instead of taking him down in front of all these people. The very thought of going anywhere with that man, even as a ruse, made my stomach twist into a knot.

I bit my bottom lip and stayed still when all I wanted to do was look up and watch the exchange between the two men.

"Understood."

James hooked his hand around my arm and started to pull me upright. "Up you go, girl."

My legs wobbled a little as I tried to balance myself on heels that were probably about two inches taller than my comfort zone.

James's hand never left my arm as we followed a few feet behind Matías.

"Do not let that man touch me," I said as quietly as possible, but loud enough that James could hear me over the thump of the music.

"He won't." He gave me a reassuring look, but I still didn't like it.

Matías pushed open a door in front of us, waiting in the hallway for us to enter first. I glanced up at the security camera, hoping like hell that Ret saw where we were going and would be here before anything happened.

"You haven't learned to keep your head down, li'l one," Matías said as I passed by him.

His voice sent chills through my body. The man was good-looking. That probably made his task easier when trying to snare his next victim. There was no way he stole them all himself, but I was sure he had a hand in more than a few disappearances.

I froze as soon as I walked inside. There

was nothing sexy or fun about this room. It was the stuff of nightmares for someone like me. I wasn't into pain. Nope. Not happening. It wasn't my bread and butter when it came to BDSM. I liked James's version with orgasm deprivation, dirty talk, and all the spankings a girl could want.

"Red," I said, fisting my hands at my side.

"No one has touched you. There's no calling red yet."

Now, that was bullshit. I could tap out anytime I wanted to, and I knew that. But in Matías's world, there was no quitting. The door slammed behind me, and Matías and James moved to my side.

James's fingers brushed against mine, and I started counting down how long it would take Ret to make it to this room before I flipped my shit. Ten seconds if Ret hustled, and he should if he valued his life.

Ten.

Matías moved toward the restraints that

hung from the ceiling, opening them and motioning for me to come forward.

Nine.

I glanced at James, waiting for his lead as to what to do next. The last thing I wanted was to be chained up and helpless with this man in the room.

Eight.

James nodded at me, and I silently cursed under my breath.

Seven.

My mouth went dry. I tried to swallow, but nothing happened. I glanced at Matías and back to James, narrowing my eyes and snarling.

Six.

I took a step forward, and Matías shook one of the shackles. I forced myself to keep moving forward when all I wanted to do was run.

Did people really do this stuff? Hand their submissive over to another person to "train"? In all my time in a club, I'd never seen it. But

Matías either wanted me that badly, or he didn't give a fuck about anything.

Five.

Three more steps and I'd be within arm's reach of Matías and the device I know he'd probably torture me with if he had the chance. My feet moved forward and I was crawling at a snail's pace, but I couldn't move any faster.

Four.

"You're only going to make this worse on yourself, girl," Matías said, growing impatient with me.

"I'm sorry." The words came out as a squeak, but hell, this was scary. I wasn't sure I'd been this scared since Rebel kidnapped me, but James was here and he wouldn't let Matías touch me. This was all for show while we waited for Ret. I repeated that in my head.

Three.

I took another step, and Matías reached out, yanking me forward. I lost my balance, tumbling toward him, and did a face plant right into his chest.

Two.

There was a loud crash as Ret came barreling through the door with his gun drawn.

One.

Matías spun me around and put me in a choke hold.

"I'll snap her neck," Matías barked right next to my ear.

Fuck my life.

I always got pulled into their shitstorm, and it never ended up like it was supposed to when we made our plan. If my dumb ass hadn't fallen forward, I wouldn't be in his arms and vulnerable.

"Fucker," I seethed and glanced over at James, who was already advancing toward us.

"One more step and it's over." Matías's grip tightened.

Ret's gaze narrowed, and his finger ticked against the trigger. He better be a damn good shot if he was going to take the chance with my head so close to Matías's. But when my legs wobbled again, I knew I couldn't be a passive victim in this.

I needed to act. The only thing I could do was to use the one thing I had at my disposal. I inched my foot to the side until it touched Matías's fancy leather shoes.

Bringing my knees up, I smashed my six-inch Louboutin down on the top of his foot. He lurched forward just enough for me to break free of his hold and run into James's arms.

"Keep him alive," James told Ret.

"Can I shoot him at least?"

Matías straightened, and his eyes grew colder. "You might as well kill me. I won't talk."

"Orders are to bring him in unharmed unless there are extenuating circumstances."

"This is extenuating." Ret smirked.

"Just let him shoot the fucker," I whispered into James's chest as I tightened my grip around his back.

James grabbed my arms, untangling me from him. "Stay here and don't move."

I wanted to cry. I needed him at that moment, but I knew I couldn't cling to him forever. If we were going to get out of here, he needed to restrain Matías.

The men worked fast, fighting Matías as they overpowered him and put him into the very shackles he was going to put me in. He screamed, struggling the entire time, but no one outside of our room could hear him.

Connor had told us every room was soundproof even though it was monitored by a two-way intercom at all times. No one would be coming to rescue Matías.

"Izzy," James said as he stalked toward me.

I was still in a haze from everything that happened, and my heart hadn't stopped pounding in my chest. "Yeah?" I whispered.

"You and Alese go back to the hotel, and we'll be back there as soon as they come to pick him up."

"Okay," I said and nodded slowly and robotically.

He wrapped his arms around me, enveloping me in his warmth and safety. "Are you okay, doll?"

"I'm okay," I said to him and buried my face into his shirt. "I'll be okay. Just a little shell-shocked."

"We would've never let anything happen to you," he said in a soft, deep voice.

"I know. Can we wait here for you? I'd rather have a drink and wait in the common area than walk back to the hotel without you."

He swept his hand across my back, soothing me. "That's fine." He leaned forward and kissed the top of my hair. "Go wait out there. Alese, if you can hear me, meet Izzy at the bar, please."

"Thanks." I hugged him tighter before breaking the embrace.

I took one last look at Matías. Seeing him helpless and restrained made me happy, but I couldn't just walk out. I needed to do one more thing to feel I had the power back.

I stalked forward, my heels clicking against the cement floor.

James turned and stared at me, but he didn't say a word.

I didn't have words for how I felt about the man, but I did have one thing I wanted to do. I raised my hand and slapped him as hard as I could. My fingernails grazed his skin as they swept across his face, leaving a red mark and drops of blood.

James looked shocked, but he didn't say anything as I spun around on my heels and marched out of the room. Fuck Matías. If I had my way, I would've tortured him until the men arrived to take him into custody. I'd hook electrodes up to his junk and electrocute him until it became useless.

Just thinking about it brought a smile to my face and gave me satisfaction. Alese was at the bar waiting for me when I walked into the public area. I slid onto the stool next to her, unhooking the leash and removing my collar.

"Fuck, that was intense."

"Sounded like it."

"Jack straight up, and keep them coming," I told the bartender.

"Same," Alese said because the girl could drink.

We'd become fast friends over the years. BDSM and ALFA were our commonalities. That, and strong men who pushed our buttons. Like me, Alese gave as good as she got.

"You okay?" she asked as I lifted my shaky hand, holding the freshly poured shot to my lips.

"I will be." I laughed. Slowly at first, but it built into a cackle.

"I'd be crying if I were you."

I poured back the Jack, taking all of it before wiping my mouth with the back of my hand. Alese looked more shell-shocked than I felt after the whole Matías ordeal. But it was over, and somehow, I'd gotten out of a sticky situation again with my life.

One thing I knew for sure—I didn't want to see the inside of a private BDSM room for a long, long time. The memory of the look on Matías's face and the panic that clawed at my insides wouldn't be leaving me anytime soon.

"Another," I told the bartender as he passed by.

I figured the best way to chase away the memory was with my buddy Jack.

17

JAMES

THE DRIVE HOME WAS QUIETER THAN USUAL. Izzy had a massive hangover and kept her eyes closed during the four hours, for fear she'd throw up all over my car. Last night, the men took two hours to arrive to haul Matías into federal custody, and Izzy had thrown back more drinks than she had in over a decade.

I carried her out, kicking and screaming, and back to the hotel room. I held her hair back as she emptied the contents of her stomach, and I gave her a bath to help her relax and clean her up. I felt like shit for putting her in the situation, and I promised myself I'd never let it happen again. Her life was too precious to me to get her mixed up in our cases.

Thomas stood in our driveway, hands on his hips, and looking a little more upset that usual.

"Hey," I said after I parked the car and climbed out.

"That was a clusterfuck, eh?" he asked.

"Nothing more than usual."

"Tommy," Izzy groaned, unfolding herself from the front seat of the Challenger in the most ungraceful way.

His eyes raked over her, and he shook his head. "You look like shit."

"I earned this hangover." She tried to crack a smile but winced. "I need my bed."

"Can we talk?" Thomas asked, rubbing the scruff on his face.

"Sure." I looked over at my wife who was

now heading toward the door. "I'll get every-thing. Go relax."

"Already doing it," she said, raising her arm, holding up two fingers.

I motioned toward the trunk with my head. The least he could do was talk while I unloaded the suitcases that barely fit in the trunk. "What's up?"

"I think, moving forward, we shouldn't involve Izzy, or any of our spouses for that matter, in any more cases."

"Already thought about that on the way home."

He raked his hands through his dark hair and sighed. "My mother already chewed me a new asshole when she found out where you two were going."

"I'm sure that was pleasant."

"I don't remember her ever being so angry with me. I swear my phone almost burst into flames."

I'd been on the receiving end of one of those

calls in the past. It wasn't fun. I hadn't thought anyone could yell louder than my mother, but I was wrong. Mrs. Gallo wasn't afraid to express herself, especially when she wasn't happy.

"It'll never happen again," I reassured him.

"She's going to want to hear it from both of us."

"I'll make a point of seeing her this week."

"Your ass better be at dinner later."

I rubbed the back of my neck, wanting to collapse in bed next to my wife and sleep until tomorrow, but that couldn't happen because it was Sunday.

"We'll be there."

"Good." He started to walk toward his bike to leave. "I'll catch you later, then."

"Give us a couple hours."

"I'll tell Ma you'll be late."

He revved the engine, lifting the kick-stand. "Bring your parents too."

I nodded as I lifted the first set of suitcases and carried them toward the house.

I needed to convince Izzy that skipping dinner at her parents' wasn't in our best interest. Well, at least, not in mine. Her mother would have my head if she didn't see Izzy was unharmed and safe.

The door opened before I stepped onto the porch, and my mother greeted me. "Welcome home." She smiled. "The kids missed you."

"Just the kids?" I asked as I walked past her and tossed the luggage on the floor.

"Us too."

"I'll be back, Ma." I kissed her on the cheek. "I have a few more bags to get."

"I don't know why you two travel with so much stuff."

That was funny. My ma didn't travel light either. She always overpacked. It was why we made them their own suite and had enough closet space and a dresser to house her various outfits.

After I'd carried everything inside, my ma asked me to have a cup of coffee with her and my father. I needed jet fuel to get me through the rest of the day, which my mother provided in the form of a Café Cubano.

Ma poured me a larger than usual cup, probably noticing the bags under my eyes from the long night. "We think we found a condo."

"Yeah? Where?"

"About ten miles away they're building a new community of free-standing condominiums, and they have one ready to move in right away."

"That's great news," I told them, lifting the cup to my lips.

"We're going to keep both places so we can travel back and forth."

That was the best news of the day. I knew they couldn't survive without our family, and this would give them the best of both worlds. Our kids would get to know them and spend quality time with them, and they'd be free to come and go as they pleased.

"We're excited," my father said.

"I can't wait to tell the boys."

I yawned. The adrenaline from the trip had started to wear off, and not even my mother's coffee could keep me awake.

"Go rest, Jimmy. We'll watch the babies."

"The Gallos would like it if you came to dinner today."

"We'd love to." My father licked his lips and rubbed his stomach. "I love her cooking."

My mother gave him the evil eye because she didn't like to be outdone. "I'll whip up something to bring."

"They'd like that," I said before walking out of the kitchen and heading up the staircase, making sure to bring a few of the bags upstairs with me.

Izzy was sprawled out on top of the comforter with her mouth hanging open. I couldn't tell if she was sleeping or passed out from the amount of alcohol still coursing through her veins.

I locked the bedroom door and stripped every piece of clothing from my body before curling up next to her. I pulled her almost on top of me, listening to her soft snores as she slept.

I could hear the faint voices of the boys playing in the backyard and the clanking of pots from the kitchen as my mother made something to bring to the Gallos'. There was a peacefulness to the noise that lulled me to sleep.

"I HAVE A BONE TO PICK WITH YOU."

I wasn't even three feet into the foyer at Izzy's parents, and her mother was already poking me in the chest.

"How dare you put her at risk?"

There was nothing I could say. She was right for yelling at me, and it wasn't anything

I hadn't already chastised myself for since last night.

"I'm sorry," I said. "It won't happen again."

She let out a loud huff, blowing a strand of hair away from her face that had fallen free from her bun. "It better not."

"I promise." I wrapped my arms around her and kissed her cheek lightly. "I love your daughter. I don't want anything to happen to her."

"If something does, I'm going to hurt you worse than you ever imagined."

I didn't doubt her words. One thing I knew about the Gallos, their word was gospel. None of them made idle threats. I'm sure if something happened to Izzy, they'd all slowly torture me until I died. That shit, I had no doubt.

"Ah, Rose." Ma Gallo turned toward my mother as soon as I let her go. "It's so nice of you to join us."

"Thank you, Maria." My ma held out a pan of flan. "I brought dessert."

Flan wasn't my thing. The slimy texture of it never sat right with me, but people went gaga over the shit. My mother's was probably the best I'd ever tasted, and I swallowed it down while smiling just for her. But only because I loved her and didn't want to end up with a hand to the back of the head.

"Come in. Come in." Ma Gallo plucked the pan from my mother's hands. "This is my favorite dessert."

My mother's face brightened as she smiled at the compliment. "Thank you, Maria. I made it just for you."

It didn't matter that they were both lying to each other. It was nice to see two of my favorite women in the same room together and happy. Although I married into this family, I was honored to call them both my mother.

"I'm going to go sit outside," Izzy said at my side with a small smile. "I need the warmth to help settle my stomach."

She needed a whole lot more than that, but whatever made her happy. "I'll check on you before dinner."

The boys ran past us, heading to the pool and stripping their clothes off before they made it through the open sliding glass door along the back of the house. They were in the water, cannonballing in for effect, before Izzy was able to take a step.

"You sure you want to go out there?" I asked her, laughing at the kids who looked more like a small army.

"I need sunshine, and the kids won't bother me."

I kissed her on the lips, dragging my thumb across her skin. "Love ya, doll."

"You too, Jimmy. Now leave me in peace for a while."

I laughed as she sashayed onto the lanai and practically collapsed in the lounge chair. She hadn't even fully stretched out when the kids surrounded her like a swarm of bees.

18

IZZY

AT THE END OF DINNER, MY MOTHER STOOD up from the table and tapped her wineglass with her spoon. "I have an announcement," she said, glancing around the table and waiting for everyone to be quiet.

The kids didn't stop outside, talking and running around the table, but she had the full attention of the adults in the dining room.

"The doctor called yesterday—yes, on a Saturday." She pursed her lips because I knew most of us were giving her a skeptical look.

"Anyway, he wanted to give me the results of the biopsy."

I sat up a little straighter, and butterflies filled my stomach. Doctors didn't call on Saturdays unless there was something really important they had to tell a patient. Right? I mean, it must be bad news if he took time out of his weekend to ring my ma. I looked around the table, and I knew my brothers well enough to know they were thinking the same damn thing. I held my breath, waiting for the other shoe to drop.

James's hand closed around mine. "Breathe, Izzy."

I squeezed his hand because no matter how hard I tried, I couldn't. I was too panic-stricken to think, let alone breathe. My body had seized, and fear set in deep in my bones.

"Anyhoo," my ma said in an upbeat voice. "He said I'm all clear."

Jesus. She could've gotten to it a little quicker than she did. I nearly passed out from an anxiety attack. She should've just said it at dinner and not made a production out of the entire thing.

I clutched my chest and sucked in a huge breath. "Thanks for almost giving me a heart attack, Ma."

Ma's face turned a beautiful shade of red, and she laughed. "Sorry. I didn't know how else to say it."

"You had me panicked," Joe admitted, rubbing his forehead before digging his fingertips into the corners of his eyes.

"Everyone just needs to be happy." She smiled.

I think she enjoyed busting our balls, but that was just plain mean. Cancer news wasn't something that should be drawn out.

"I love you, Ma," I told her, and everyone followed suit.

"She's my girl. She can't leave me yet," Pop said, wrapping an arm around my mother's waist.

Dessert was served with a little more enthusiasm than usual. Everyone had been feeling the weight of the impending test results for a solid week, and now that we knew she was clear, it was like a weight had been lifted off our shoulders.

"Who wants to join me outside to eat?" Max asked, staring straight at me.

"I guess I do," I said, grabbing my plate from the table.

"Me too." Suzy started toward the lanai and was joined by Mia.

I knew exactly what this was about. Mike told Mia, and she made the phone calls, telling everyone that I had lied. I knew the word was out about Kat before I'd even stepped foot in the house. When I woke up in Jacksonville this morning, there were thirty-seven texts in our group message.

I ignored every single one of them because there wasn't a point in arguing via text. I knew I'd get my ass chewed out today anyway; why prolong the agony? They needed to get over their shit and quick. We'd already hired Kat, and her first day of work was tomorrow. There was no way in hell I'd let them derail anything.

"So," Max said, smacking her lips together and tapping her foot against the pavers. "Do you have something to tell us?"

I sat down, brushing the hair from my eyes before staring straight at her. "I don't know what you mean."

"About Kat. You know," Suzy said, being her cute, innocent, and sometimes clueless self.

"She starts tomorrow."

"And does she lick pussy or not?" Max got right to the point.

I leaned back in the chair and clutched the armrests. "I didn't ask."

"Mike said she doesn't," Mia barked out.

"Mike probably doesn't know what day it is," I reminded her as I pointed at my head with a shitty smirk. "Listen, bitches. I don't care if she sucks cock, eats pussy, or fucks a dog. She's a damn good artist, and we're lucky to have her at Inked."

Max scoffed and so did Mia, but Suzy nodded.

"Maybe you should meet her before you condemn her to being a trollop who'll steal your middle-aged husbands."

"Our men are hot as fuck," Suzy said.

I almost fell backward, toppling from my chair, at her words. I so loved dirty-mouthed Suzy, but she didn't always make an appearance.

"Bravo on the perfect use of the word, babe." Mia reached across the table and gave Suzy a high five.

"Well, it's true." Suzy looked pleased with herself.

"Isn't Inked's birthday coming up?" Mia asked.

"Yeah. Next week." I'd totally forgotten about it. Typically, we had some sort of party to celebrate, but with everything going on, it was the last thing on my mind.

"I'm planning a party, and we can all meet Kat together," Max announced.

"Fine." I gave in. They weren't going to let the whole Kat thing go until they met her for themselves and realized they were being ridiculous.

"So, it is said. So, it shall be done," Suzy said and finally relaxed back into her chair.

"Where did all the kids go?" Mia asked after the entire troop ran inside.

"Who knows? Just enjoy the moment of quiet."

I was talking about the girls more than the kids, but I wasn't going to say it. My headache from drinking hadn't waned, and being around my family and their loud voices didn't do a damn thing to help.

Suzy stuffed a huge bite of flan in her mouth and moaned. "This is amazing."

"Hmm." The way I felt, flan would push me over the edge and have me running to the bathroom to hurl into the porcelain goddess. "Glad you like it."

"I need to get the recipe," she said as she licked the spoon.

"Suzy." I rolled my eyes.

"What?" Her forehead wrinkled as she frowned, glancing around the table as we all laughed.

"Let's be real, sweetie."

"Shut up, Izzy. I'm a better cook."

"Yes. Yes, you are. You no longer burn Ragu," I snickered.

Max tapped on her screen a few times. "Next Saturday night. I posted the party invite online already. It's set."

"Well, we didn't even run it by the guys."

"I always plan the party," she said, and she did a bang-up job of it.

Last year, the fire department showed up because we were over capacity. It was one of the biggest parties in our town, and people talked about it for weeks.

"Got the tent too for overflow."

"Smart," Mia said.

I laid my head back, watching the overhead ceiling fan swirl in circles before I closed my eyes to enjoy the slight breeze. For spring, it was hotter than Hades on my parents' lanai. With little wind, the humid air was more stagnant than usual.

I couldn't wait to get home to the air conditioning and put this day to an end. I wanted my boring life back, getting back to the grind at work and alone time with my husband and kids.

Sometimes it was easy to forget it was the little things and the quiet times that meant the most. Adventure and danger didn't interest me anymore. I was too old for that shit anyway. I was content with my life, and I decided I'd do everything in my power to keep it calm on the home front. We were at the point where we needed to spend more time together and less time working. Kat would make it happen for me, but what could I do to convince James to dial it back too?

<hr>

THE THIRD TIME THE ALARM WENT OFF, I

rolled onto my back and groaned. "Do we have to get up already?"

"I feel like all we do is work," James said, moving to my side and sliding his hand over my stomach.

I dug my fingers into his hair, twirling it between my fingertips. "I think we need to start taking time off. The kids are growing so fast, baby. We're missing so much."

"It'll be summer soon, and they'll be off school."

"Maybe we can cut down to four days a week at work."

"Sure, doll. That's not a problem. You have Kat starting, and maybe we can bring on some new guys at ALFA so I can cut back my hours."

I smiled down at him. "Thank you."

I couldn't believe it was so easy to convince workaholic James to cut down. But maybe he felt like me…time was slipping away from us. In the end, we weren't thankful for all the hours we worked. We were reminded of the moments we spent together, or we were filled with regret.

He looked up. "For what?"

"For agreeing."

"There's nothing more important than you and the boys, Iz."

I let out a contented sigh and closed my eyes. "Just five more minutes," I begged.

The bed dipped, and James settled between my legs. "That's all I need, baby."

I wrapped my arms around his neck and lifted my head to kiss him. "Imagine all the mornings we could do this," I told him.

"Then let's quit."

"Don't be silly," I laughed. "Fuck me. You're down to four."

"I only need three," he said with a smirk.

"That's nothing to be proud of, sweetie."

He pushed inside of me, filling every inch of me. I moaned, resting my hands on his ass because I loved to feel it flex underneath my touch as he pumped into me. He gave me a solid minute of slow lovemaking before he pounded into me like a madman working against the clock.

When we orgasmed and collapsed, he rolled onto his back and rested his hands on his chest. "Fuck, quickies aren't as fun as they used to be."

I ran my fingers through the damp hair on his chest. "You're getting old." I chuckled.

"Speak for yourself. Now you must pay," he said, pulling me down and pinning me to the bed.

"No, don't," I begged. "I can't walk around all day all worked up. I'll kill someone."

"No butt plug?" He pouted.

"You ever want to be fucked again?"

Like the smart man he was, James gave in and let me off the hook. Literally. I didn't have to walk around all day with something shoved up my ass just so he could get his rocks off all day thinking about it. Sure, I loved a good punishment and the anticipation of him fucking me later, but today wasn't the day. Especially not after the weekend we'd had.

By the time I made it downstairs, James's mother had the boys ready for school and standing at the door to kiss me goodbye.

Trace had on his favorite Transformer shirt and denim shorts with a pair of matching high-top sneakers. Mello and Rocco had on whatever I left on their dressers. They were past the stage where they cared about how they looked and were too young to think about dressing nice for the girls.

I knew the day was coming. The girls who would coo over them and chase them through the schoolyard, but thankfully, it was still a ways away.

"Bye, Mama," Rocco said, standing on his tiptoes to give me a kiss on the cheek.

I ran my fingers through his buzz cut, loving the feel of it under my palm as he winced.

"Ma," he groaned.

"Shush it," I told him, doing it again because I fucking could.

"You can touch my hair, Mama," Mello said, pushing Rocco out of the way.

My twin boys were so opposite of each other. They were both tough and growing like weeds. Soon, they'd be taller than me. But Mello was the gentler, kinder soul. He still loved to snuggle up to me on the couch and watch a movie. Whereas Rocco wanted his own chair like he owned the joint. He was more like his father in that way.

I did the same thing to Mello's hair as I did to Rocco's, but Mello smiled. "Love you, Ma."

"Love you too, baby." I kissed his soft cheek, inhaling his smell and wishing he still had that newborn scent.

"Trace, be good today. No calls from the teacher this week, okay?"

Trace smiled as his face turned red. "I promise."

The boy promised me the moon but

rarely ever delivered. I basically was on a first-name basis with his teacher. She loved him to death and probably let him get away with more than she really should. Trace knew it too. But every once in a while, he pushed the envelope a little too hard, and she'd have to call me to reel him in.

The last time I had a meeting with her, I learned Trace was caught tapping a little girl's ass as he'd said, "Good girl."

I was mortified when I found out. I had to hear an entire spiel about hands and how that could be construed as a sexual act. They wanted him to attend a sexual harassment class, but I pitched a fit because he's a fricking kid. He was too young to even realize what it meant, but I knew where he got it. The school overstepped its bounds, but obviously, I had failed as a parent. It didn't help that he didn't have any sisters to interact with so he was kind of clueless as to what was appropriate or not.

After that, I told James to keep his hands

off my ass and watch it with the sexy talk in front of Trace. Obviously, I didn't want a repeat performance because James would be fielding that meeting, not me.

"Let me grab my purse, and I'll take you to school."

James's mother came walking out of the kitchen with her purse already over her shoulder. "I'll take them, dear. Sit and have a cup of coffee. You need to learn to relax a little more."

From her lips to God's ears.

"Thank you, Mama."

"Yay," Rocco yelled and ran out the front door. "Shotgun."

"Darn it," Mello grumbled and followed him.

Trace looked at me and shrugged. "I like the back seat. I don't understand the big deal."

"That's good, baby." I blew him a kiss. "Be good."

"You got it, doll." He winked and ran out the front door.

I stood there shocked. All I'd wanted was one girl. But, no. God had to punish me for being such an asshole most of my life. Instead, he gave me three boys who would probably be the death of me someday. If not that, they'd at least make me gray before my time.

I didn't even want to think about what was to come. Besides the girls, there were going to be parties, drinking, driving, and probably an arrest or two before they hit adulthood. I'd be lying if I said I was looking forward to any of it.

"We may be gone by the time you get home. We're going back to Miami, but we'll be back in about a month to check on the house."

I hugged Mama Caldo tightly. "Thank you," I told her before kissing her face. "I couldn't have gotten through the week without you."

"I loved spending time with you and the boys."

I knew she was including James along with the grandkids, and it made me smile. "They loved it too."

"Go have your coffee and give my son a kiss goodbye for me."

I waved as she walked down the driveway toward the car with the boys already fighting inside. "I will."

I closed the door, pressing my back against it. I took in the silence because I knew it was my last few moments of quiet before I headed to work and a very long day training a new girl in the way of Mike's crazy.

19

JAMES

I WALKED INTO THE OFFICE JUST AFTER EIGHT and Angel had already set a cup of coffee in my office, but she was nowhere to be found. The hallways weren't buzzing with activity, but I was too tired to even care.

I collapsed in my chair, turned on my computer, and sipped the still warm coffee as I waited for the old piece of shit to start. The door to the conference room down the hall from me opened and closed before Thomas appeared in my doorway.

"Feds are here." He tipped his head. "They want to talk to both of us."

"Is it bad?" I asked as I stood from my chair, leaving my coffee behind.

"They wouldn't say. They wanted to talk about Matías."

I growled slightly as I followed Thomas to the conference room at the end of the hallway. We were only hired to find the man. After that was done, we should've been finished. Being at ALFA a little after eight in the morning on a Monday didn't sit well with me.

"We're both here," Thomas said as I walked in behind him and closed the door.

I sat down across from a female agent in a pressed black pinstripe suit and looking nothing like the sexy ones in the movies. I still hadn't found a single one who looked like Jennifer Garner or Angelina Jolie, but it didn't stop me from hoping.

"Thank you for joining us, Mr. Caldo."

"You showed up unannounced, and I own

this company along with Mr. Gallo. You're lucky I'm here at all."

I don't know what it was about her statement, but it didn't sound like she was giving me a compliment. I hated fuckers who acted like you owed them something just because they carried a badge.

"What can we help you with?" Thomas asked, giving me the side-eye.

"We wanted to fill you in on Matías and hand-deliver the reward."

"Is something wrong with Matías?"

She shook her head and cracked a smile. "Amazingly, he's spilling his guts."

I laughed. The fucker said he'd never talk. "Interesting."

"We found out he isn't really the head of the operation. He's only the face, and there's someone more important that we need to catch."

"Need help?"

They weren't able to do what we did with Matías because they had to get warrants and wait for bureaucratic red tape; whereas we could follow a lead and use any means necessary to find the man.

"We may. We'll see how far we get with him in custody. Hopefully, he'll give us everything we need to find the real culprit and put him behind bars."

"You're not going to let him off, are you?" Thomas asked the first thing that popped into my mind as she finished speaking.

"No. Matías will spend the rest of his life in prison. His cooperation will determine if he's given a posh facility or goes to supermax."

He shouldn't even have that option. The man deserved to be ass-raped every day, repeatedly, by a group of men that made him call them "Daddy." The government always did bullshit things like this to get people to cooperate. While I understood it, I didn't like it.

The agent slid an envelope across the table and tapped on it with her fingernail. "As promised. There's a check for one million dollars made out to ALFA to cover your expenses and as a reward."

"Thank you." I smiled and pulled the small, nondescript white envelope in front of me. "We appreciated the chance to serve our country again."

It was nice to work on something other than cheating wives or business partners who stole money from each other. But I didn't think I wanted to get involved in another case like Matías's. The government should learn to handle their own shit without looking to outsiders to help.

"We won't keep you. I'm sure you have important things to do today."

"We do, but we appreciate you delivering the check personally," Thomas said, standing to shake the hand of the agents.

"The pleasure was mine." The woman nodded, releasing his hand and expecting the same from me.

"Thanks for this," I said, waving the check

in the air, but not bothering to stand and thank her for it.

I was in a pissy mood, and she was taking the brunt of it. I didn't know if it was because it was Monday or that I had to leave Izzy after such a clusterfuck of a weekend.

After Angel escorted the agents out, Thomas closed the door and smiled. An emotion he didn't always do so easily. "Open the fucker."

I tore open the envelope, pulling out the million-dollar check. "It looks real."

"Dude, that's a lot of bank for a case we basically worked on for a week. What are we going to do with it?"

"You can do whatever you want with your part, but with mine, I'm taking a lot of time off this summer. So, I'll use it to hire a new person and cover their payroll for a while."

He knocked on the table, his knuckles crushing into the wood. "Why?"

"I need to spend time with Izzy and the boys. I promised Izzy we'd do things this summer before time got away from us. You should think about doing the same."

He sat down across from me and folded his hands together. "Angel and I have been talking about it too."

I wasn't surprised. All we did was work. Izzy, at least, had slightly different hours at Inked, which gave us some leeway. But with Thomas and Angel both working at ALFA, they didn't have that luxury.

"Let's throw the whole thing in the company kitty and hire some new people so we can enjoy our families a little more."

I rubbed my chin and suddenly felt a headache coming on. "Who are we going to leave in charge when we're not here?"

"Bear or Morgan. They know the business best."

"Bear?" I almost choked. He was the most senior, but the man fucked around so much, I wondered if he'd take the job seriously enough.

"What's going to work better? Morgan

telling Bear what to do, or Bear telling Morgan what to do?" Thomas quirked an eyebrow.

"Frisco, it is," I said and started to laugh.

"It's a shame Flash isn't going to be around. I would've had him handle shit in our absence."

"Yeah," I said and found I actually missed the little pissant.

He'd only been gone a few days, and his absence had already been felt. Skyping him and email conversations weren't the same as seeing his face around the office and having someone to argue with. But I understood why he was home and supported him one hundred percent.

"Frisco will be a great middleman."

I nodded my agreement. "When do you want to tell them?"

"Not until we have to. I don't want to listen to Bear's mouth for the next two months."

"Good idea."

"And if the Feds come back?"

"Fuck them. I'm done doing their dirty work."

"I'm with ya, buddy."

As long as we were both on board with turning down any further assignments the government had to offer, I was down for whatever cases came rolling in between now and summer. I'd cut my hours and do exactly as I'd promised Izzy. I'd spend more time with the people I loved most.

20

IZZY

Kat was early and was waiting outside Inked when I arrived. She had an oversized Betsey Johnson purse slung over her shoulder and was texting on her phone as she paced in front of the doorway, wearing a pair of ripped denim capris, wedge heels, and a classic eighties rocker tank top.

"Good morning," I said as I walked toward the door, fumbling with my keys to find the right one to unlock the shop. I was still dragging ass, even after ingesting two cups of Mrs. Caldo's Cuban coffee.

She turned to me, jamming her phone in her pocket. "Morning, Izzy."

"Are you ready for today?"

"I've been training for this my entire life."

I giggled softly as I unlocked the front door. "The guys are excited for you to join us, but not more than I am. It's nice that we'll have another girl in the shop because it's been hell on me being the only chick."

She followed me inside, looking around the shop like she'd never been here before. "I don't know how you did it. I couldn't work with my brothers."

"I love them and have learned how to handle them," I told her as we walked into the back area to start our prep. "They aren't so bad once you get to know them, but they can be a bit…" I trailed off.

"Bossy?" she answered.

"Yep."

"I'm honored to help bring up the chick count around here."

"I appreciate it more than you'll ever

know. Here's your station." I pointed to the empty one next to mine because there was no way I was putting her closer to anyone else.

"Mind if I put a few personal things out to make it feel more like home?"

"Knock yourself out," I told her before bringing my purse and a box of donuts I'd brought into the back room. I started the coffeepot and turned on the music because, although I loved silence at times, I couldn't stand it at the shop.

By the time I walked back into the work area, Kat had set out a few decorations and pinned a couple pictures to the wall.

"I hope this is okay," she said as she looked at her setup and smiled. "I like to have my good luck charms around me."

I walked over to her station and took in her display of two troll dolls, a backstage pass, a tiny inspirational plaque, and two photographs. "Who's in the pictures?"

She pointed to the one that was clearly her family and rattled off their names. Her brothers were handsome devils, and her sister looked like a miniature version of hers. "These are my parents, Sam and Nancy. They own a small bar on the beach in Clearwater."

She looked to be the only tattooed rocker chick in the family. Everyone else looked like buttoned-up professionals. "And your brothers?"

"Park is a lawyer for a fancy law firm in Tampa, and Jasper is finishing his residency at USF and will soon be a full-fledged doctor." She glanced toward the ceiling. "Lord help us. His ego is already too big."

"And your sister?"

"Juniper owns a small boutique in St. Petersburg that sells the trendiest clothes and trinkets and makes a killing off the tourists."

"They all look so…"

She turned to me with a smile, the cat eyes she painted on this morning becoming more pronounced. "Normal?"

I nodded because she took the words right out of my mouth.

"Yeah. I'm the one who always tended to be a little outside the norm."

"All the Gallos are freaks, so I can't imagine what that was like for you."

"Eh, it was no big deal. We love each other for our differences. Most of the time, at least."

I touched the last photo, which was of a band playing on stage and had one of the hottest men I'd ever seen holding a microphone. I couldn't mistake the face. Cypress McDermot was the lead singer for the most popular rock band in the country. They'd been burning up the charts for the last six months, and I saw their faces plastered everywhere. "You're a fan, I assume?"

Her smile turned into a smirk. "He's my boyfriend."

My body rocked backward, and my mouth dropped open. "You're dating him?" I pointed at the photo, shocked.

"Uh, yeah. Fucking him too." She giggled.

"Well, damn, girl. Get on with your bad self."

I started to laugh and couldn't stop. "I'm sorry." I waved my hands, wondering if my sisters-in-law would back the fuck up once they heard that little nugget of goodness. If she was getting a piece of ass like Cypress, there was no way she'd be trying to steal a fortysomething tattoo artist from the middle-of-nowhere Florida.

Her smile faded. "Is it that hard to believe?"

"No," I said quickly. "You two make a killer couple. It's just that…" I didn't know how to put it without sounding like a complete cunt, so I just said it. "My sisters-in-law were…" I couldn't even finish the sentence because it was so ridiculous at that point.

She started to laugh, realizing what the hell I was talking about. "I do not want your brothers. Not that older men aren't attractive, but come on, I'm twenty years younger than them, and I'm not a homewrecker."

"They're just afraid of the unknown."

"I get it. I worry every day when Cypress is on the road. Pussy is being hurled at him from every direction." She leaned back in her chair and turned it from side to side, gripping the leather seat. "I trust him, though. Maybe I'm stupid, but I can't worry about what he's going to do. Either he loves me, or he doesn't."

"When did you two meet?" Suddenly, I was fangirling and wanted a sneak peek into the world of Cypress McDermot.

"We went to school together and were high school sweethearts."

"Ahh, you'll be the one he marries," I told her because that's how it always worked out when someone found fame and people were trying to be with them for reasons other than love.

"You think?"

I nodded with a big smirk. "Trust me. I

know these things. You loved him when he was a nobody. Now, everyone wants him, but they don't know the real him. But you know him. You love him. You'll be hitched in no time."

The front door chimed as the guys arrived. "We're here." Mike's voice echoed through the shop, loud enough that we could clearly hear him over the music.

"We're in the back," I yelled back. I turned to her. "Don't let anything they say get to you."

She nodded at me before the three men strolled into the work area. "I got this."

"I'm sure you do."

"Kat." Joe gave her a quick chin lift and went immediately to his station to start setting up.

Mike had the appointment book in hand, prepping for his tiny powwow that was supposed to get us pumped on a Monday morning. Anthony, for once, didn't have his phone out and his face buried in it.

"Good morning," Mike said, tucking the appointment book under his arm. "I see you're all set up."

Kat smiled at him. "I'm ready to kick some ass."

"We have a team meeting at least once a week before the clients start to arrive. I always try to keep it short and to the point."

Anthony muttered "Bullshit" under his breath.

Joe rolled his eyes and whispered something none of us could hear, while I laughed my ass off.

"Make it quick, Mike. None of your rambling shit today."

Ten minutes later, the meeting was over, and Mike clapped his hands, giving us some mumbo jumbo to pump us up. All four of us just stared at him as he gave us his best Tony Little impression, telling us how we could "do it."

"Kat, you already have two clients booked today. Great start."

"Thank you." She smiled at him. "I just want to say how honored I am to be here and be a member at Inked. It's been my dream since I was a kid."

I almost spat out my coffee when the guys' faces dropped. I didn't think they realized we were all getting older. Now the kids had us as role models. We weren't the cool kids. We were middle-aged but still killing it.

"Since you were a kid?" Anthony asked with a look of horror on his face.

"Yeah, I was like ten when I came in here with my uncle. I was so in love with the vibe and you guys that I knew I had to come back someday."

"Ten?" Mike ran his hand through his hair and blew out a puff of air.

"Yep." She smirked.

I wanted to clap, give her my approval for knocking them down a peg or two because that shit was funny as fuck.

"Well, I…"

"Dudes, we're old. Get the fuck over yourself," Joe barked because he was the only one who didn't have his head up his own ass most of the time.

"One last order of business." Mike cleared his throat, flexing his muscles a few times, but it didn't work on Kat. "We're having our annual celebration on Saturday evening. Max will be stopping in this week to go over the details, but she's planning the entire thing. Just make sure to tell everyone who comes in this week about it and post that shit on your social media."

"Yes, sir," I said, being a smartass because, duh, we knew what to do.

"Now, let's get to work." He stalked off toward the front counter.

"That was intense," Kat said with a big smile.

"He's just getting started, kid," Joe told her. "Just wait."

"Do you listen to everything he says? Like do you follow it to a T?"

"Fuck no. The man was hit one too many

times. He babbles sometimes and thinks he's the boss. Just follow our lead," I told her and she nodded.

This was going to work out just perfectly. Not only was Kat a kick-ass tattoo artist, she was dating one of the sexiest rockers on the planet, and she was going to be my new work bestie. Girls had to stick together, especially when we were outnumbered.

Saturday, when the girls found out Kat was dating Cypress, they were going to shit a brick and hopefully feel like a giant bag of dicks for all their bullshit. I knew they thought their husbands were the sexiest man ever to roam the earth, but Kat had snagged a real prize, and there was no way any of the Gallos were going to make her toss it all aside for a little cock.

"Hey," Kat said as she started prepping her station for her first client. "Can I bring a guest Saturday?"

"Sure," Anthony told her as he finally

pulled out his phone, going back into isolation mode. "Who?"

"My boyfriend."

"Cool," Joe said, but none of them had any idea who that boyfriend was except me.

Max, Suzy, and Mia were going to pass out when Kat showed up with Cypress on her arm. I couldn't wait to see the looks on their faces.

Sometimes those cunty bitches needed a reality check. I couldn't wait for the cold, hard truth—or the sexy hot body of Cypress—to slap them back into reality.

Saturday couldn't come fast enough.

21

JAMES

"I can't believe you talked me into this dumb shit." I pulled my fishing pole out of the water and tossed it behind me.

"You gotta learn to relax," Mike said before taking a sip of his lukewarm beer.

We'd been ten miles off the coast of Florida, sitting in the middle of goddamn nowhere, bouncing on the waves of the Gulf of Mexico for three hours and hadn't caught one fish. Not one. Not even a minnow nipped at our lines. All we'd accomplished was blowing through a shit-ton of beer and almost getting sunburned.

"This is better than working," Thomas said, pulling on his line as if there might be something on the other end.

Joe kicked his feet up on the edge, leaning back in one of the captain's chairs that lined the side of the boat. "I needed a day away from the women. They're acting weird this week."

"Just this week?" I laughed. Izzy wasn't acting weird, not after finding out her mother was cancer-free.

But I knew exactly what Joe was referencing. Izzy had told me about the shitstorm hiring Kat had created with the other women in the family.

"Anyone know what's going on?" Anthony asked. "I can't figure it out."

The man, God I loved him, but sometimes he was clueless. Usually because he was too busy or self-absorbed to realize what was happening in plain sight, but it still boggled my mind.

"Who knows. I don't even let it bother me. All I know is that Mia dropped to her knees and sucked me off the other day as soon as I walked in the door from work." Mike grunted and thrust his hips. "Shit was hot too."

"I wish Max would do that. All I get is the damn stink-eye."

"Angel isn't acting weird at all. Is Izzy?"

I shook my head, but I kept my mouth shut.

"You two are fucking lucky. It's been like PMS Central at my place," Anthony added.

I stretched out across the leather bench at the front of the boat, soaking up the sunshine and listening to the steady waves lapping against the side of the boat. "What's changed in the last week or so?"

I felt like I should at least throw them a bone out of loyalty and being brotherly and shit. I knew I'd want to figure the shit out sooner rather than later if I were in their shoes.

Mike let out a loud sigh before raking his hands through his hair. "Nothing."

"You sure?" Thomas finally reeled in his line and gave up just like I had.

Joe scratched his head. "Kat?"

Ding. Ding. Ding. We have a winner. At least one of the brothers had some sense left in his head to figure it out.

"You think they're upset about her?" Anthony asked Joe.

Joe shrugged. "I don't understand why they would be."

"Nah, that can't be it." Mike pursed his lips. "They're not jealous."

Thomas walked behind Mike and smacked him on the back of the head. "Don't be a dumbass. They feel threatened."

"So I got sucked off because Mia was threatened by Kat being near?" He looked even more confused than before.

"Bingo," I said, throwing my arm over my face to block out the sunlight.

"Fuck. I don't want her to feel that way, but I also want another surprise blowy."

"Did you really just call it a blowy? Are you fucking five?" Anthony barked and started to laugh hysterically.

"Shut up, asshole," Mike growled. "How are we going to fix this?"

"We'd better start paying more attention to our ladies," Joe told them.

"Um," Anthony mumbled. "If I pay any more attention to Max, I might as well crawl up her ass."

"Still not getting any anal from her, huh?" Joe teased and made a *tsk-tsk* noise.

"Fucker, that shit is locked up tighter than Fort Knox."

"You lost your game, my man." Joe laughed.

"Why did we ever come out here?"

"To fish," Thomas reminded Anthony.

"I came out to get away from the insanity and drink."

"We've accomplished that, but it looks like a storm's rolling in soon, and I feel the need to remind my woman who owns her," Joe said, tossing his fishing pole aside. "Who's with me?"

"Maybe I'll get a blowy tonight too," Anthony teased.

"Fuck that. I'm going straight for the ass. No better time to play the anal card than right now." Mike collapsed next to me. "You with me, man?"

"Always, brother," I muttered under my arm. "You're a beast."

"Take us home, Thomas," Joe said from across the boat. "I have a woman to please."

At least one of them had some sense. While Mike and Anthony wanted to use the situation to their advantage, my other brother-in-law had his head on straight. He knew the way to make his woman feel better about the entire Kat situation was to shower her with attention and remind her how much she meant to him. The other guys…they were greedy fuckers, but they did love their wives too.

By the time we made it to shore, a storm had indeed rolled in, and tethering the boat to the dock wasn't so easy. But I had a feeling the hard work for the men around me was just beginning. They talked a big game, but the women in their lives were the bosses, leading them around by their dicks.

EPILOGUE

"Where's Kat?" Max asked within one minute of stepping into Inked on Saturday.

"She's off today," I told her, secretly jumping for joy on the inside because Max was chomping at the bit to see her.

"Damn it. How do I miss her every time? She'd better have her ass at the party."

When Max had stopped in earlier in the week, she'd texted me that she was on her way. Kat didn't have any clients, so I told her to take off early and do some errands to pick up some supplies for the shop. Really, I just wanted to piss Max off, and it worked like a charm.

"She'll be here."

"Fine," she grumbled and placed her hands on her hips. "If she doesn't show…"

"Shut up. She'll be here."

"Mmm-hmm. Well, anyway, the tent is going up now, and the caterers will be here any minute. We only have two hours until the party starts."

Max should've hooked up with Mike. They would've been a powerhouse couple of anxiety and bossiness. I giggled at the thought because I didn't know who would've come out unscathed in that marriage.

The entire Gallo clan came walking in the shop like a small army, ready to put Max's plans into action. They lined up like a troop as Max started to rattle off job duties to make this party happen.

Within hours, the inside of Inked was transformed into a spectacular party space, and the tent was filled with tables and chairs along with a DJ.

"You went all out this year," I told Max, impressed with her skills on such short notice.

"It has to be bigger and badder than last year, girl." Max smiled, looking around at everything we'd accomplished in a short time under her watchful eye.

"I guess so. You did it."

Anthony strolled up next to Max and put his arm around her shoulder. "Everything looks amazing, baby."

She snuggled into his side and wrapped her arm around his back. "Thanks. I'd do anything for you."

"Even anal?" I quirked an eyebrow, which earned me a very sour and unhappy glance from Max.

"Anal? Really? That would be amazing," Anthony said. "You sure know how to spoil a guy."

"Fuck you, Izzy, and you too, Anthony."

She pulled away from him and glared at him. "You know how I feel about that."

He grabbed her hips and pulled her close. "You love when I put my finger in there." He waggled his eyebrows, and her face reddened. "My dick isn't much different.

"I can't," I said and walked away.

Max laid into him something fierce. I couldn't stop laughing. Poor Max. She always liked to seem like she was in control, and Anthony always had a way to throw her off-balance. I think it was why they worked so well.

Suzy tugged me off to the side. "Are you sure she's coming?"

"I'm sure."

She pulled at her top lip and gave me a halfhearted smile. "Okay. I trust you."

I rolled my eyes and walked over to Joe. "Handle your woman," I told him before I went to find where James had wandered off to.

He was sitting in the shop, occupying my chair as Thomas sat across from him, and they were talking about business. What else would they talk about?

I slid into James's lap and ran my fingers through his hair. "No talking about work tonight. Got me?" I glanced between the two of them. "This is a work-free zone."

"Said the woman who's still at work," Thomas replied with a slight smile.

"It may be where I work, but tonight is all about fun," I reminded him. "Anyway, I thought you two were going to cut back a little."

James tightened his grip on my ass and nuzzled his lips against my neck. "We were just talking about some applications we received this week."

"You're going to hire new people?" I gawked at him.

He nodded and winked. "I made a promise, doll, and I intend to keep it."

"You've made me a happy girl." I kissed his lips, holding his face in my hands as I did it.

"We're both going to cut back at work and spend more time with our families," Thomas said.

"If you need help, I can go through your applications," I offered.

Thomas and James laughed.

"We've got this," James told me. "You worry about your business, and we'll handle ours."

Burn. "You're lucky I love you so much."

"I am." James squeezed my ass tighter. "There's no one else I could ever love more."

"Not even Sofia Vergara?"

He thought about it for a minute until I hit him. "Not even her."

"Good answer." I kissed his lips again before hopping to my feet. "Outside, both of you. No hiding and no work."

"You're the boss," Thomas said.

James patted my ass with a twinkle in his eye that said "I am going to get some later" as he passed by. I checked my hair and makeup and locked up the office before joining the rest of the crew under the tent.

Thankfully, we'd found two babysitters who would watch the kids tonight. We paid them twice their normal rate because of the number of kids and the short notice. By now, the two girls had to be ready to pull their hair out, but I was sure it was nothing they couldn't handle.

As soon as I went back outside, I sat down with Suzy, Max, Mia, and Angel, along with Ma, at a table under the tent. Even though the sun had almost set, it was blazing hot, and I didn't want to start sweating before anyone arrived. There was nothing worse than hugging and kissing on someone who was stickier than the morning grass.

A motorcycle pulled into the parking lot, Kat's long hair blowing in the breeze as she clutched the man on the front. From a distance, it would have been hard to tell who was on the bike with her if I didn't know any better. His dirty-blond hair was going every which way but forward, and his sunglasses hid his signature green eyes perfectly.

"Well, she's not a lesbian," Max said with pursed lips.

"Nope." I smiled.

"But at least she has a man," Suzy said, always trying to stay optimistic.

I was dying for this moment. There had been so many times this week that I'd wanted to spill the secret, but it was just too good not to be there to see their faces when Cypress was standing right in front of them.

"Maybe they're just friends with benefits," Mia quipped and shrugged her shoulder.

"For the love of God. You guys need to zip it."

Kat climbed off, her hands on Cypress's shoulder as she bent forward and shook her hair out. She had wild, messy hair that looked like she'd just gotten fucked, and she looked more beautiful than normal.

"Couldn't hire an ugly bitch, could ya?" Max barked.

"She's not that pretty." Suzy sighed. "Is she?"

"No. Not unless you're into the big tits, long hair, and killer body thing. What guy wants that?" Angel said, yanking everyone's chain and earning a laugh from me.

Cypress pulled Kat closer, pressing her tits against his chest and kissing her lips while he stayed seated on the bike. He whispered something in her ear, and she tipped her head back and laughed.

"I hate her," Suzy said. "I want to be that young again."

"Can't go back, girl. Do you really want to do your early twenties all over again?" I asked because I sure as hell didn't.

"I want to start over right when I met your brother on the side of the road."

"Yeah," I said, remembering the night I met James.

The man swept me off my feet. At least, that's what I told the kids. They never needed to know their father and I had a one-night stand, and I hadn't wanted to see his mug after that. He'd chased, though, and I was powerless to resist his charms. Who was I kidding? He was relentless, and he kicked ass in bed. Charm was an entirely different story.

When Cypress climbed off his bike and stretched, I pictured him on stage, microphone in hand and the crowd cheering around him. He had it. That quality that commanded the attention of everyone in the room. The girls around me saw it; they were drawn in and couldn't stop staring. At least they weren't glaring at Kat anymore.

When he took off his sunglasses, I knew they recognized him immediately. You would have had to have been blind not to notice his eyes, and the band T-shirt was a dead giveaway.

"Is that…?" Suzy leaned forward and squinted.

"Can't be." Max's mouth dropped open, and for the first time in forever, she was rendered speechless.

"Oh. My. God," Mia whispered.

"Holy fuck." Angel started to choke on her drink.

"Yep, bitches. It is."

I sat back, watching them eye-fuck Cypress and completely forget about the girl on his arm.

"God, he's even better looking in person." Mia lifted her glass to her forehead, feeling the heat but not from the sun. "I couldn't handle all that."

"I'd sure as fuck try," Max said quickly. "Hell, maybe I'd let him do my ass too."

Suzy snorted, and a little bit of her drink dribbled down her chin. "Shit. I'm going to look a mess when I meet him." She dabbed at the spots on her tank top and growled.

"What about your husbands?" I asked, crossing my arms in front of my chest, filled with satisfaction.

"They're fine." Max pointed behind her. "They're over there."

"Why didn't you tell us she was dating Cypress McDermot?"

I cackled. "Because I couldn't miss seeing your sour pusses when you realized what idiots you've been."

"We're not idiots. We're careful." Mia shot me a shut the fuck up look.

"You really think Kat wants a guy in his forties with a wife and a gaggle of kids running around?"

"Hell, right now, I don't even want that when he's this close." Max waved her hand in front of her face, fanning herself. "He's just so…"

"Yeah," Suzy sighed. "All that."

"What's everyone looking at?" Anthony asked, coming up behind Max and following her line of sight.

"Max said she'd give you anal, Anth." I laughed, and Max shot me daggers.

"Holy shit. Is that the dude from…" Anthony snapped his fingers together and closed his eyes in deep thought.

"Yep. He's the lead singer of Wicked Innocence."

"Dumbest name ever," Anthony mumbled.

"Doesn't matter. They made it. They could be called Wicked Shit as long as people are buying," I told him because he was just jealous he had never made it to the same level as Cypress, even though he'd tried like hell.

"He's coming," Max said. "How do I look?" She glanced up at Anthony.

He rolled his eyes. "Lookin' like you owe me some ass with this display you're putting on."

Max growled and turned back around just as Cypress and Kat came to a stop in front of our table. Cypress smiled, his dreamy signature smile. The bedroom eyes with their emerald green flare weren't believable unless I saw them in person. Now that I had, I was a bit awestruck.

Kat placed her hand on Cypress's, which

was resting on her shoulder. "Cy, this is Izzy. The one I was telling you about."

Cy—yeah, I'm on a first-name basis now—looked every bit the rocker with his torn jeans, black boots, and band T-shirt. He extended his hand to me and said, "Hey, Izzy. It's a pleasure to finally meet you."

I chuckled like a complete idiot. "The pleasure is mine," I said, sliding my hand into his palm and thinking if I were twenty years younger... But then James wouldn't be around and neither would my three adorable and rambunctious little boys.

"Cy flew in this morning because he wanted to meet the crew."

Max lifted her hand, wanting and needing attention. "I'm Max."

Anthony shoved his hand over Max's head before Cypress had a chance to take it. "I'm Anthony, Max's husband and part owner of Inked."

"Right..." Cypress said with a smile. "Kat told me you used to have a band."

"I did. We were quite successful in the area. Never had your kind of fame, but then again, I fell in love with this one." His eyes dipped to Max. "And decided I'd settle down first."

I had to bite my lip to stop myself from laughing. He'd never had Cypress's kind of fame because although Anthony had an amazing voice, the rest of the band sucked sweaty balls. Meeting Max and settling down just gave him a reason to leave the band without feeling like an asshole.

"Smart move, man. Touring is the worst." Cypress frowned. "I've never felt so tired in my life."

Mia pulled out the chair next to her and smiled up at Cypress. "Why don't you sit down?"

The behavior of my sisters-in-law would be almost appalling if it weren't so obvious and downright funny. They could've almost mothered this man, yet their cougar sides came out and they wanted to climb him like a tree.

"Yo, Mike and Joe. Come over here," I yelled toward the guys.

"There goes the party," Suzy mumbled, to which Angel smacked her.

"Hey, you work in an office filled with hotness," Suzy snapped back.

Joe and Mike stalked over and said hello to Kat and shook her boyfriend's hand.

"What's up?" Joe said to him, playing it cool.

"Yo," Mike said, in typical Mike fashion.

"Do you know who that is?" Suzy said, trying to whisper but failing.

"No." Joe looked confused as his eyes scanned Cypress. "Kat's guy. I saw a photo in the shop." He shrugged.

"He's Cypress."

"Okay," Joe laughed. "Hi, Cypress."

"You're impossible." Suzy rolled her eyes. "You know, from Wicked Innocence."

"Is that a store?" Joe asked Suzy with a straight face.

"Dude." Mike hit Joe in the stomach with the back of his hand. "You know, that band. We hear them all the time on the radio at the shop."

"Kinda," Joe muttered. "Cool, man. Congrats."

"Wait a second." Cypress raked his hands through his hair, looking as impressed as we did with him. "Are you Iceman?"

Mike's face transformed with a huge smile. "I was."

"Fuck," Cypress said, looking down at Kat. "I saw this guy fight when I was a kid. He's a beast, baby. I can't believe you're working with him now."

Kat shrugged, probably not giving a fuck about fighting just like the rest of us. "That's cool."

"I'm honored to meet you, sir." Cypress held out his hand, and Mike shook it quickly but with a little bit of a frown.

"It wasn't that long ago, kid."

Mike went from being on top of the world at being recognized to being reminded that he was an old bastard within thirty seconds.

I hopped out of my chair and hooked my arm with Kat's. "Let me introduce you to everyone else before our guests arrive. This is Angel, my sister-in-law, who's married to my brother Thomas."

They both shook Angel's hand, and she blushed the brightest shade of red when she touched Cypress. These girls couldn't keep their shit together in front of him, and it was embarrassing.

"James." I touched his shoulder, and he turned with a smile.

"What's up, doll?" He slid his arm around my back and stared at Cypress and Kat.

"This is Kat and her beau, Cypress."

"It's nice to meet you," they both said, but not at the same time.

"Did you have a good first week at Inked?" James asked, making small talk, which wasn't always his strong suit, but he'd gotten better. I had to give him brownie points for trying harder for me too.

"It was amazing. I've never worked anywhere that felt like home so quickly." Kat beamed. "Your wife has been so helpful. She's really an amazing person."

James nuzzled my neck. "She really is. I'm a lucky man."

"Aren't they cute, honey? I want to be like them when we're old."

James growled in my ear, "I'm sure you will be."

And just like Mike, they reminded me I was no longer the hot young thing I used to be either. I was a mom and a wife and not the wild Izzy who ended up in the back of police cars with bikers hot on my trail.

"Let me go finish the introductions, and I'll come join you for a drink," I told James.

"I'll wait here for you." He patted my ass again as I walked away with Cypress and Kat in tow.

"Thomas." I motioned between Kat and Cypress. "This is Kat, our new artist, and her boyfriend, Cypress."

"It's nice to meet you both. Don't let the group scare you away. They're harmless."

"You have an amazing family."

"Thomas doesn't work at Inked. He and James own a private investigation agency."

"That's good to know." Cypress reached out for Thomas's hand. "Never know when I could use your services."

"We're always here to help." Thomas smiled. "Well, I'd better get to my wife."

"We'll catch you in a bit," I told him and turned to face the cute young couple. "Feel free to wander around, or do whatever you want."

"Thanks, Izzy." Kat smiled, pulling Cypress closer to her body.

With her tucked under his arm, they looked like the most beautiful couple in the world. I could almost see them walking the red carpet at the Grammys someday. At least I could say I knew her when.

"If the buzz gets too much, feel free to duck out whenever."

"We're staying for the whole party. I miss home," Cypress said. "I told some of my buddies to stop up here too. I hope you don't mind."

I shook my head, but I was a little bit panicked we wouldn't have enough alcohol and space once word spread that *the* Cypress Mc-Dermot from Wicked Innocence was here. "Don't mind at all," I lied because I wasn't about to tell the celebrity standing in front of me that I wasn't sure how I felt.

After I greeted a few guests and made my presence known, I started to search for James, but I couldn't find him anywhere.

I pulled out my phone and did what any normal person would do in the same circumstances. I texted him.

Me: Where are you?

I covered my eyes, blocking out the sun,

and glanced around the parking lot again, but no James.

James: Office.

I stomped toward the office, wondering what the hell he was doing in there when the party was happening outside. "Hello," I yelled as I walked through the lobby toward the office tucked away in the back.

"In here," James yelled on the other side of the door.

I rolled my eyes, ready to chew his ass out, but when I opened the door to find my husband with his pants pulled down and the biggest hard-on, stroking it with a look in his eye that said I was about to be thoroughly fucked, I forgot everything.

It had been ages since we'd done it in the office, worried that we'd get caught. I suddenly didn't care that we had a tent full of people. They wouldn't miss us.

"Close the door," James commanded.

I pushed it closed with my ass and walked

toward him as I unbuttoned my jeans. "You want this?"

"I want you."

His deep voice sent sparks of electricity shooting through my body. I walked toward him slowly, unzipping my pants when his arm reached out and pulled me forward.

"You're moving too slow," he said, flipping me around and yanking my pants down so fast that I almost lost my breath.

I leaned forward, flattening my body against the desk, dizzy with anticipation. When his hand caressed my ass, I moaned and wiggled my ass, ready for him to thrust into me.

But James pressed his body flat against mine, placing his mouth next to my ear. "You want my cock?"

"Yes," I whispered.

"You want me to fuck you?"

"Yes." I sealed my eyes shut and smiled, giddy with excitement.

"I need to be inside you," he growled,

rubbing the tip of his dick against my opening. "I need it more than air."

"Fuck me," I begged, panting and ready.

James pushed into me, taking me with slow strokes as his hands slid underneath my tank top and gripped my waist.

"Touch yourself," he said. "I want to feel you come on my cock."

I reached between my legs and stroked my clit as he thrust into me. The desk hit the wall with each blow, pushing me closer to the edge and toward the orgasm I hadn't even known I wanted until I walked through the door.

"Faster." I pushed my ass back and thrust my cunt at him, wanting more of him.

He grunted, taking me deeper and harder than before. Within minutes, I was tumbling over the edge, gasping for air and riding the high.

I loved my life. I loved my husband. I loved my kids. There wasn't a thing I would change. Not a moment I would alter because it wouldn't bring me to this very second, tucked away in the office with James. Where the future would bring us, I didn't know, but I sure as hell was excited to find out.

THANK YOU FOR READING **WORSHIP ME!** *I hope you loved the Gallo Family. But don't worry - the family's story continues!*

There's two spin-off series with the Gallos and they're waiting to be devoured.

If you love James and Thomas, ALFA Investigations. ***Download your FREE copy here!*** The series is sexy and suspenseful and filled with your favorite characters too!

Looking for more Gallo family dinners and insanely hot alphas?

Check out the Men of Inked: Southside and get to know the other side of the Gallo family. One-click Maneuver and download your copy now!

AND SIGN UP FOR MY NEWSLETTER TO FIND out about new books… *menofinked.com/news*

You can also join my Facebook group, *Chelle Bliss Books*, for exclusive giveaways and sneak peeks of future books.

I appreciate you help in spreading the word, including telling a friend. Word of mouth is everything.

Reviews help readers find books too! Please leave a review on your favorite book site.

My entire audiobook collection is available on your audio retailer. Tap here to see where you can download your next favorite listen.

MEN OF INKED: SOUTHSIDE SERIES

Join the Chicago Gallo Family with their strong alphas, sassy women, and tons of fun.

- Book 1 - Maneuver (Lucio)
- Book 2 - Flow (Daphne)
- Book 3 - Hook (Angelo)
- Book 4 - Hustle (Vinnie)
- Book 5 - Love (Angelo)

MEN OF INKED SERIES

"One of the sexiest series of all-time"

-Bookbub Reviewers

Download book 1 for FREE!

- Book 1 - Throttle Me (Joe aka City)
- Book 2 - Hook Me (Mike)
- Book 3 - Resist Me (Izzy)

- Book 4 - Uncover Me (Thomas)
- Book 5 - Without Me (Anthony)
- Book 6 - Honor Me (City)
- Book 7 - Worship Me (Izzy)

ALFA INVESTIGATIONS SERIES

Wickedly hot alphas with tons of heart pounding suspense!

- Book 1 - Sinful Intent (Morgan)
- Book 2 - Unlawful Desire (Frisco)
- Book 3 - Wicked Impulse (Bear)
- Book 4 - Guilty Sin (Ret)

SINGLE READS

- Mend
- Enshrine
- Misadventures of a City Girl
- Misadventures with a Speed Demon
- Rebound (Flash aka Sam)
- Top Bottom Switch (Ret)

NAILED DOWN SERIES

- Book 1 - Nailed Down
- Book 2 - Tied Down
- Book 3 - Kneel Down

TAKEOVER DUET

What happens when you sleep with your biggest enemy?

- Book 1 - Acquisition
- Book 2 - Merger

FILTHY SERIES

- Dirty Work
- Dirty Secret
- Dirty Defiance

LOVE AT LAST SERIES

- Book 1 - Untangle Me
- Book 2 - Kayden

BOX SETS & COLLECTIONS

- Men of Inked Volume 1
- Men of Inked Volume 2
- Love at Last Series
- ALFA Investigations Series
- Filthy Series
- Takeover Duet

View Chelle's entire collection of books at menofinked.com/books

To learn more about Chelle's books visit *menofinked.com* or *chellebliss.com*

ABOUT THE AUTHOR

Chelle Bliss is the *Wall Street Journal* and *USA Today* bestselling author of Men of Inked: Southside Series, Misadventures of a City Girl, the Men of Inked, and ALFA Investigations series.

She hails from the Midwest, but currently lives near the beach even though she hates sand. She's a full-time writer, time-waster extraordinaire, social media addict, coffee fiend, and ex history teacher.

She loves spending time with her two cats, alpha boyfriend, and chatting with readers. To learn more about Chelle, please visit menofinked.com or chellebliss.com.

JOIN MY NEWSLETTER

Text Notifications (US only)
➜ Text **BLISS** to **24587**

WHERE TO FOLLOW CHELLE:

WEBSITE | TWITTER | FACEBOOK | INSTAGRAM
JOIN MY PRIVATE FACEBOOK GROUP

Want to drop me a line?
authorchellebliss@gmail.com
www.chellebliss.com

facebook.com/authorchellebliss1

bookbub.com/authors/chelle-bliss

instagram.com/authorchellebliss

twitter.com/ChelleBliss1

ACKNOWLEDGMENTS

I don't even know where to begin. Writing Worship Me was a whirlwind and made my head spin.

First and foremost, thank you to every reader that was patient with me during this time. I know it's been a long time since I've released, but your support has meant the world to me.

www.ingramcontent.com/pod-product-compliance
Lightning Source LLC
Chambersburg PA
CBHW051207190726
48288CB00006B/1852